M000158172

PUMPKINS & POLTERGEISTS

Confessions of a Closet Medium, Book 1

NYX HALLIWELL

Beach
Path
Publishing

Pumpkins & Poltergeists, Confessions of a Closet Medium, Book 1

© 2020 Nyx Halliwell

ISBN: 978-1-948686-28-0

Print ISBN: 978-1-948686-26-6

Cover Art by EDH Graphics

Formatting by Beach Path Publishing, LLC

Editing by Trish Milburn, Patricia Essex

By payment of required fees, you have been granted the non-exclusive, non-transferable right to access and read the text of this eBook. No part of this text may be reproduced, transmitted, downloaded, decompiled, reverse engineered, or stored in or introduced into any information storage and retrieval system, in any form or by any means, whether electronic or mechanical, now known or hereinafter invented without the express written permission of copyright owner.

Please Note

This is a work of fiction. Names, characters, places, and incidents are either the product of the author's imagination or used fictitiously, and any resemblance to actual persons, living or dead, business establishments, events or locales is entirely coincidental.

The reverse engineering, uploading, and/or distributing of this eBook via the internet or via any other means without the permission of the copyright owner is illegal and punishable by law. Please purchase only authorized electronic editions, and do not participate in or encourage electronic piracy of copyrighted materials. Your support of the author's rights is appreciated.

"Built into you is an internal guidance system
That shows you the way home.
All you need to do is heed the voice."
~ Neale Donald Walsh

Chapter One

The summons to "come home" to Thornhollow arrives on a cloudy, drizzly day in October.

These types of missives normally come from Mama, but the scented lavender envelope is addressed to me in my Aunt Wilhelmina Rae's handwriting.

In her sixties, she is a spitfire of a woman, and her wild penmanship is beautiful in its bold strokes. I can almost hear her voice as I tap the envelope on the table and wonder what's inside.

It's been a long day at the bridal salon and my feet are killing me. Setting the rest of the mail on the table, I turn the tea kettle on. Then I kick off my high heels and rub my toes.

Arthur and Lancelot, my gray tabbies, emerge from their hiding places to greet me with meows and chin rubs against my bare calves. I scratch each behind his ears, fill their bowls with kibble, and shrug off my sweater, hanging the damp garment on the back of a chair to dry.

As the water heats, I head to my bedroom to shed my business attire and replace it with my favorite flannel pajamas.

There's no one but me and the cats, and they don't care if I'm in my comfy clothes at six o'clock on a Friday night.

Back in the kitchen, I absentmindedly tie my fuzzy robe around me and make a cup of mint tea. A slice of leftover pizza calls to me from the fridge, and I settle down with both to sort through the bills and junk mail. Once again my eye catches on the lavender envelope. Mama has no doubt recruited her sister to convince me to move back home.

Being an executive bridal consultant at Southern Bridal Flair Salon pays well and I enjoy the work, but every once in a while I wish I'd followed my dream to be a wedding dress designer. To live and work out of my aunt's old Victorian house with its warm woodwork and welcoming open rooms. I long thought I'd one day become a partner in her event planning business, The Wedding Chapel.

Running my finger over the edge of the envelope, I feel the tug to return to Thornhollow and the comfort of my childhood. I have good memories there, but also the pressure to live up to my mother's political and social aspirations. At least here in Atlanta, I'm surrounded by designer and couture dresses every day and not plagued by small-town gossip. Maybe one day I'll get up the courage to show Darinda, my boss and the owner of the entire Southern Bridal Flair chain of stores, my sketches.

The scent of Aunt Willa's perfume drifts up from the stationary as I tear open the envelope and slide out her letter.

The Wedding Chapel is embossed in flourishes at the top, with her business address, phone number and website underneath. Merely adding a website this year created enough drama with her that I nearly let it go. But convincing her to move into the modern age and reach beyond Thornhollow for customers was a good step. She's already increased business ten percent since I set up the website in April.

Her Southern graces are evident even in her penmanship.

. . .

My Dearest Avalon,

I'm afraid it's time for you to return home. Danger is afoot. Innocent people are getting hurt.

I sip my tea and frown, rereading those words before continuing. What danger could there be in our sleepy town?

I've done my best to protect our family and Thornhollow from the curse, but I'm afraid I cannot do it on my own for much longer. It's time for you to stop pretending you're normal and use your gifts in the way in which the universe intended.
All my love,
Aunt Willa.

Perhaps it's the shadows of the evening closing in or the quiet of my apartment, but I find myself pulling my robe a little closer. While I scrutinize the letter several more times, it doesn't make her message any clearer. What danger? A curse? Why has she been protecting the family and the town from it? What gifts of mine is she referring to?

Okay, I know that answer, but no way I'm delving into the ghost world.

Most importantly, why the heck didn't she just call me?

I sip tea, rub my temples, and feel a smidge of frustration at the cryptic note. She and Mama have a definite flair for melodrama.

In the foyer, I dig my cell out of my purse and see that I've missed a call from my mother. My tired frustration vanishes for a second. *Protecting the family.* Is our family actually in danger? From what exactly?

My mother is mayor of Thornhollow, and while she's had

her share of people who dislike her politics, she's on friendly terms with everyone. Plus, she typically calls me twice a day, so seeing a missed call from her shouldn't trigger panic.

It does. I carry the phone back to the kitchen and plunk it on the table, debating whether to jump into my family's craziness again or not. It's one of the reasons I had to leave Thornhollow —they were making me crazy, too.

Aunt Willa is probably the least crazy of any of them, even though my mother claims the opposite. "Willa Rae is vexed," she used to proclaim. She then would spin her finger around her temple indicating mental instability. "You can't believe a thing she says."

I resume my seat, finish off the pizza, and open the rest of the mail. The kitchen grows dim, and I get up to turn on the light.

When I flick the switch nothing happens. The kitchen stays steeped in darkness. That's when I realize the lighted numbers of the microwave clock are out, and the living room ceiling fan has stopped spinning.

Stupid wiring. I've complained to the landlord multiple times about the fluky electricity, as well as the plumbing that bangs and rattles at all hours of the day and night. The house is a hundred years old and some of that is to be expected, I guess, but it's extremely frustrating when this stuff happens.

I reach for the phone and feel a breeze pass over my hand. Aunt Willa's letter sails off the table, the breeze rocking it gently back and forth, like a leaf falling form a tree, before it lands on the floor.

Goosebumps race over my skin. Pressure and a high-pitched ringing starts in my ears. I look around for the cats, but they've disappeared.

"Avalon..."

The voice sounds like it's right behind me. I whirl but see nothing except shadows.

Shaking my head, I pick up the letter, returning it to the table. As I reach for my phone, it rings, the sound blaring in the kitchen and startling me.

It's my mother again. "Hi, Mama," I answer, forcing a deep, calming breath. "I just got home from work. Can I call you back in a few minutes?"

I swear I feel that breeze again tickle the back of my neck. My gaze falls on the letter and the words *danger is afoot.*

"Oh, Ava," Mama sobs, her voice shaking with tears. "You have to come home."

The hair on the back of my neck shoots straight up. "What happened?"

Another choked sob. An audible intake of breath. "Willa Rae is dead."

Chapter Two

The usual three-hour drive to Thornhollow is dark and rainy, filled with road construction and a washed-out bridge, causing it to take nearly five. Arthur is bedded down in the passenger seat, Lancelot in my lap. I focus on the road and give into my grief, listening to a variety of late-night radio talk shows, while I weep.

As I turn off the highway populated with signs for peaches, boiled peanuts, and the various wineries in the area, the sorrow comes rolling back. My chest tightens, hot tears build in my eyes. I haven't been home in months, but it feels like years.

Victorian era street lamps softly illuminate Main Street, the numerous buildings from another time period, stately and regal, as I wind my way north to Mama's. At the far end is the crossroad where The Wedding Chapel—Aunt Willa's home and business—occupies the corner. She owns over an acre, the ground sloping toward the creek at the back, with limestone hills and woods on the side.

As I pass her large painted lady, I see light seeping from an upstairs window—the bedroom I used to call my own.

Another spasm hits my chest, and a tear slides down my

cheek. It's as if Aunt Willa has left a light on for me. Silly, of course, and yet I almost stop to see if someone is inside. Probably Rosie, her assistant, accidentally left it on.

I don't think I'm ready to go in and see my beloved aunt's things, smell her perfume, or speak to anyone yet, so I keep going, chilled and exhausted.

Arriving at Mama's, all the lights are on. She lives in a mid-century craftsman. This is not the house I grew up in, but it suits my mother. She thrives in this space filled with thick oak, stained glass windows, nooks for her endless books, and multiple beautiful fireplaces. The deep front porch showcases stately rocking chairs, pumpkins, and fall mums.

Since she's mayor and my aunt's death is big news in our town, reporters—all two of them—are camped outside wanting a statement. As I exit the car, both speak to me on my way to the front door, offering sympathy since they knew Aunt Willa as well.

They don't ask me to make a comment, but I see the way they take in the pajama legs under my trench coat, my red nose and swollen eye. I did nothing more than throw a few clothes in an overnight bag, grabbed the cats, and headed here. Thankfully, neither of these two is interested in taking my picture.

The front door flies open as I climb the steps, and Mama grabs me off the porch. My hands are full of the cats, so I'm not able to hug her back as she embraces me, crying softly. Once inside, with the door shut, I put down Arthur and Lancelot, and Mama steps back to look me over.

"Why Ava," she chastises, "what in the world are you wearing? Your picture will be all over the *Thornhollow Tribune* tomorrow."

Even at this time of night, she's dressed in conservative attire, somewhere between a casual suit and silk pajamas. I can't quite decide which. Her hair is in a perfect coif of graying blond curls, and her makeup is demure but perfect.

"I imagine the *Trib* has more important news to report on than the state of my clothes in the middle of the night after my aunt has died."

She clucks her tongue, and that's the message that the state of my dress could affect her upcoming campaign. I'm not sure she even realizes she's in that mode all the time, even when her sister has just died, because running for office has become her life.

Her eyes are bloodshot, her nose chapped. Her voice hitches as she talks a mile a minute while directing me to the kitchen. She doesn't even ask if I would like a cup of tea, simply starts heating the water and pulling cans of loose flavors from the cabinet. As the cats roam, getting reacquainted with her house, I shed my coat.

"They think Willa's heart stopped and she fell into the creek," Mama says, dashing at the tears springing to life again and rolling down her cheeks.

Dropping dead from a heart attack is not the worst way to go, I think, but of course I can't speak it out loud. Wilhelmina Duchamp was too young to die. Falling in the creek, though...

I shiver, thinking about my poor aunt.

"She was having a few issues, you know, but Doc thought it was angina. Panic attacks." She places a cup on a saucer and digs out a flowery sugar bowl from the pantry to place on the table. "Ever since we were kids, she fought with buckets of anxiety. I just don't know."

I pull out a chair and sit. "Don't know what?"

She waves a hand through the air as the kettle whistles. She doesn't ask what flavor I want, picking one for me. "I can't believe she's gone."

I can tell there's more to this, but Mama's having a dose of understandable anxiety herself and that's why her mind isn't tracking straight. "I never realized Aunt Willa had heart problems." I try not to sound annoyed no one bothered to tell me. "When did this start?"

She brings the tea and sets it in front of me, steam rising. "You haven't been home in a while."

This is an accusation, a condemnation, and an explanation all in one. She fiddles with her fingers, rubbing each in turn, her gaze skittering around the kitchen. "I was there."

"What?"

Her eyes bounce to me then away. She peers into her lap. "I think I heard her arguing with someone right before it happened."

I reach over to still her nervous finger twitching. "Mama, what are you talking about?"

She grips my hand like a steel vise and sighs audibly. "We were going out for an early dinner. I had a city council meeting and Willa had a bridal appointment, but she wanted to talk to me about something. Said it was important. When I arrived, she wasn't in the house. I figured she was out back, prepping something for the bridal appointment. You know how she loves to show the place off, so the bride gets a feeling for what it would be like to marry in the gardens. I went out on the back porch and…"

The tension in her body washes through me. I see fear in her eyes. Her grip grows stronger still.

"It's okay, Mama," I cajole. How many times in my life have I had to do this? Talk her off the ledge so I can get into her head long enough to figure out what's going on in there. "Just tell me what happened."

"I heard her voice, and it was that argumentative tone that she likes to take. I figured someone was already back there with her. They were too far away to actually hear what was being said, and it seemed to be coming from the old Thornton Homestead."

The homestead is the original home of Sam Thornton and

Tabitha Holloway built on the creek bank. My distant ancestors founded this town. The home is a historic landmark at the edge of the property but fell into disrepair long before I was born.

Mama's tension seeps into my central nervous system. I gently urge her to continue again.

Another deep breath racks her body. "I didn't hear the other person. It was odd, but like I said, I couldn't understand what they were saying. Really, all I heard was Willa Rae. She was upset, though. And then I got a phone call from Queenie and went back inside to answer it. When I was done, Willa Rae was still outside, so I went to look for her. I never saw anyone...and then I found her."

The way her voice softens and trails off, the way her eyes look so sad, I realize the truth. Mama found Aunt Willa dead in the creek.

"I'm so sorry." I give her hand another squeeze. "That must have been terrible for you."

Tears wash down her face as she meets my eyes. "She was face down in the water. If I'd gotten there a little sooner..."

"There was probably nothing you could have done, Mama, even if you did get out there sooner."

But I can see in Mama's eyes that she's thinking the same thing I'm wondering in the back of my head. "I told them about the arguing." Her voice drops to a whisper. "What if she didn't have a heart attack, Ava? What if..."

"Who did you tell?"

She gets up as if she can't sit still a minute longer and paces to the sink. There, she begins washing out a dirty glass. "The police promised to look into it. But since I didn't hear anyone else or see who it might have been, they're not concerned about it. Everyone loved your aunt, so maybe they're right. Who knows? Willa Rae often talked to herself. Maybe there wasn't someone else there."

Conflicting emotions war inside my heart. Snatches of the letter float through my brain.

Danger is afoot.

Oh, Aunt Willa. What happened?

It's nearly sunrise before I get the reporters to leave and soothe Mama enough to get her to bed. Doc has prescribed some gentle sleep meds for her, and once those kick in, I know there's not much else I can do.

I gather up the cats, and we head to Aunt Willa's.

Chapter Three

❦

A sticky gloom wraps Aunt Willa's house like a blanket, as if the life of the three-thousand-square-foot mansion died when she did.

I park at the curb. The front porch and grounds showcase her flamboyant decorating skills, covered in pumpkins in all shapes and sizes. Mums in burgundy, orange, and white add pops of color, surrounded by gathered and tethered corn stalks.

The lawn, bleached by the hoar frost, is enclosed with a black wrought iron fence, a fleur de lis on the top of each waist-high spike. A miniature wagon sits in the front yard, kissed with frost, holding hay bales and gourds.

The wide, wrap-around front porch is decked in garlands of fall leaves, weaving around the white columns. The two large windows on the first floor are filled with a display of what appears to be a woodland wedding, complete with gnomes with red hats and a bridal Snow White. Over the door is The Wedding Chapel sign showcasing the business in white letters. The *Sorry, we're closed!* notice hangs limply from its hanger inside the glass door.

Leaving Arthur and Lance in the car, I cringe when the

ornate gate lets out a hair-raising squeak as I tug it open. The ground is damp and smells of wet leaves and fresh soil, the big magnolia tree near the sidewalk dripping water from a brief shower an hour ago.

Plop, plop, plop. Fat drops fall, a couple landing on my head, as I take the stone-paved walkway to the house. The eastern sky eases into a pink-tinged gray, and everything is veiled in a dull pallor of fog.

I don't plan to stay long, just enough to check on Tabitha, my aunt's cat, and make sure the place is locked up tight. I also have an urge to walk down to the creek, near the old homestead, in order to see if I can find any trace of Aunt Willa and her possible guest.

Did Mama imagine it? Was Aunt Willa simply chiding Tabitha or one of the dozens of wild animals she often fed? Was there actually someone with her when she died? If so, why didn't they try to save her?

A sickening thought, and subsequent chill, ripple through me. *No,* I tell myself. *No one in Thornhollow would ever do my aunt harm.*

At the top of each porch railing sits a gargoyle-shaped black cat. Part of the original house, the twins suit it perfectly for this time of year. Growing up, my aunt always told trick-or-treaters to pet the cats' heads for good luck. I stroke the top of one of them when I reach the top step, an old habit.

A fake apple has rolled off the cornucopia display on the nearby wicker table. Picking it up, I realize it's real, a slight bruise blooming on its highly polished red skin where it smacked the wooden floor boards when it fell. Aunt Willa must have just created or freshened up the display in the past day or so.

My heart squeezes at the thought of her bustling around, creating the beautiful display and smiling over it. Fall was her favorite season, and she reveled in the decorations.

The emotions I've been holding back in order to be strong for my mother crash over me. "Oh, Aunt Wilhelmina, what happened to you?"

For a heartbeat, the air seems to shimmer. "She was murdered," a raspy voice says on my left.

I jump, dropping the apple.

It rolls toward the steps, my pulse skidding with it. I whirl to face the sidewalk and street.

There's no one there.

"Hello?" I scan the yard, the mass of woods on my right, Mr. Uphill's place on the left. The last of the night has given up to the rising sun, but all I see is the murky fog covering trees, a few bushes, and the empty street.

Plop, plop, plop, the rain resumes, falling lazily and rolling off the porch roof. I scan the entire yard again, more slowly this time, and the well-manicured flower beds edging the porch. Mums, green ferns, trailing ivy, and jasmine plants covered with fake spiderwebs sit quietly, the murkiness of the morning making everything heavy.

"Over here," the thin, raspy voice says, and I jump again, turning toward the sound.

It's coming from the door.

I edge closer, narrowing my eyes. The antique knocker—a cat head that matches the gargoyles—licks its lips.

My feet scramble backward and I blink. Then shake my head as if I can clear my vision by doing so. The foggy gloom is playing tricks with my eyesight, that's all. The voice?

Um, yeah. I'm hearing things, too.

While everything in me wants to run, I ignore the flight instinct, move closer once more and peer at the knocker. "Hello?"

The antique cat head, complete with pointy ears, doesn't change this time. It doesn't move at all, even though I sense it's watching me back. When it doesn't reply, I blow out a sigh of relief. Straightening, I chuckle at myself. "You're losing it," I reprimand myself. "Totally bonkers."

And then the cat's lips curve in a snarky smile. "You going to stand there all day and talk to yourself, or are you going to go in?"

I'm so freaked out, I leap like a jackrabbit, feet scrambling, arms flying, in an attempt to get off the porch.

Something rolls under my right foot and I fall, cartwheeling through the air. My feet fly up, the rest of me careening down. For a moment, I'm suspended, all three gargoyle cats watching with amused expressions, and my butt smacks the bottom step.

The wayward apple, also thrown into the air, lands on my stomach as my head whacks hard on the stone walk.

Pain like an ice pick ricochets through my skull. Above me, the last star blinks out in the sky as rain dampens my skin.

But the stars on the edges of my vision are bright and hot, until everything whites out in a brilliant flash, and I plunge into darkness.

Chapter Four

Lazy mist wraps around me, clouding my vision. I swear it's thick enough to taste and sticks to my skin like cotton candy. My body feels light as a feather.

"Ava?"

I turn in a circle, the voice so familiar it hurts. "Aunt Willa?"

Heavy silence meets my ears. My mind must be playing tricks on me again. *Aunt Willa is dead,* I remind myself.

"*Aaavaa...*" The voice again, whispering as if it's flying right past me. It's definitely my aunt's.

Just a dream.

The dream takes shape, though, and the mist parts. Her face appears. "The trunk in your bedroom—there's a false bottom..."

She swims in and out of the soupy air, as if something is trying to pull her away. I step forward, lifting a hand to reach for her. "Come back!"

She does, her upper body coming into a hazy focus. "All you need is inside, Ava."

My hand goes through her. "Need for what?" My voice seems to echo against the mist in the air, bouncing back to me.

"My armoire...secret compartment..." Her voice drifts, her face begins to fade again. "Push the top left cor..."

My logical brain kicks in. "Aunt Willa, you know you're..."

I can't say it.

"Dead," she supplies. "Yes, I know, dear. Don't you cry for me, now, sweet girl. You're not dead, and you have to..."

She fades again.

"Have to what?" I'm losing her. Grief floods me. "Oh please, Aunt Willa! Come back!"

"In the attic," her voice drifts past me, incorporeal. "The book..."

I lose her again, but a few feet away I see the outline of her. Her head turns to her left to look at something. I squint in that direction as well but see nothing but the cotton candy fog.

"I have to go." She looks over her shoulder at me. "It's up to you, Ava. I love *youuuu.*"

She fades away.

"No!" I yell.

And then I hear her voice once more, "Now wake up!"

A heavy weight depresses my chest, hard and fast, shoving the air from my lungs. Once, twice—

It stops, and then out of nowhere, I feel the warmth of lips against mine. My mouth is open, breath rushing in. I taste mint and...

"Dead, is she?" a raspy voice asks.

"Not anymore," another answers, and I recognize them.

I gasp, eyes flying open.

I'm still on the ground, wet and cold. The most beautiful cornflower blue eyes are looking down on me.

"Ava?"

The man's face comes into sharp contrast. Tousled hair the color of toasted pecans, classic nose, tanned skin. He's clean-shaven and the smell of his faint aftershave fills my nostrils as I inhale a huge gasp again. For half a second, I see the boy he used to be floating under the man he is now. "Logan?"

Relief is like a washcloth wiping the worry from his brow. He sits back, blows out a breath between his lips, and rakes his hand over his face. "You just took ten years off my life."

I wonder if I'm still in the dream or whatever it was. Logan Cross. What is he doing here?

The sky above his head is golden now with the rising sun, pale strips of peach streaking across the sky between clouds. His face blurs, and I see two of him. My ears ring with a coarse blare that makes me flinch. "What happened?" I ask.

"You tell me." He keeps a firm hand on my shoulder to stop my struggle to rise. I feel something warm and slippery drop onto my hand, and see a basset hound on my right. His sad eyes stare at me as another string of drool slides out of his mouth. "Mox and I were just coming back from our run. I saw you fall off the porch. By the time I got here, you weren't breathing, and I thought you were dead."

"Dead?" The memory of the fall sends fresh pain from my head down to the base of my spine.

The blare in my ears grows louder, but it's not from the head injury. It's a siren.

I draw a deep breath, reassuring myself I'm very much alive, and a new pain hits. I'm going to have a sore rib cage from the CPR he was administering.

The feel of his hands on my chest, his lips on my mouth, surfaces, causing my head to throb and my heart to kick. As a teen, I dreamed of Logan Cross's attention. I would have died, figuratively, to have his lips on mine.

"Told you," one of the voices I heard earlier says.

I tilt my chin to look toward the porch. The cat gargoyles at the top of the bannister stare back, the rising sun reflecting in their eyes and making them glow. One's lips move ever so slightly. "She's alive."

The basset hound turns his head, as if he hears them as well, before he looks back to me.

I struggle to come up onto my elbows, ignoring all the various waves of pain, as an ambulance, siren blaring, careens to a stop at the curb.

"EMTs are here," Logan says, as if it's not obvious. "Stay put."

Logan Cross is a lawyer these days. The only one in Thornhollow. A good one from what I've heard. His parents run the famous Cross Winery north of town, and his brother has a brewery two towns over. For whatever reason, Logan decided to go a different direction with his life, and his office is directly across the street from The Wedding Chapel.

People in Thornhollow either come from old money, like Logan, or they survive at the other end of the spectrum, like Reverend Stout. He rushes up to us with a plastic medic's box and plunks down beside me.

Gray-haired and wrinkled, he's wearing a white shirt and navy pants, a name tag penned over a pocket of the shirt that has a protector filled with pens and a tiny flashlight. Today he's an EMT, working on physical bodies rather than souls. "Second time I've been here in the last twelve hours," he murmurs in his deep Southern voice. His gaze rests on my face and softens. "Ava Fantome, my goodness, young lady. What in the world happened? So sorry about your aunty."

Logan tells him what he knows—he saw me trip, fall down the steps, and hit my head. When he reached me, I wasn't breathing.

I interject a few details, trying not to sound like a scatterbrain or klutz. Neither man seems to listen.

"Thank the Good Lord you were here," Stout says to Logan. "We might have lost her, too."

"I wasn't dead," I insist, but the voice in my head casts doubt. *Was I?* "I did have a weird dream though."

"Did you see a bright light? Go down a tunnel?" the pastor

asks.

"No. I saw my…"

Logan and Stout stare at me.

"Never mind." I wave it off. "I'm fine. I fainted, that's all."

Reverend Stout's partner rolls a gurney through the yard, bumping over the limestone pavers. Stout flashes his light in both of my eyes, declares I might have a concussion, and they insist on carting me to the hospital.

A flurry of activity continues around me. A police officer arrives—in Thornhollow anytime the ambulance is called out the police are, too. Preston Uphill, the owner of the B&B next door, runs over in a tartan-colored robe and slippers. I sense others gathering on the sidewalk outside the gate, their voices a background hum.

"Avalon?" Uphill calls. "Oh my goodness, are you okay?"

"Just tripped." I push up to sitting and Logan grabs me as my vision blurs and I nearly tip over. "I'm fine."

"Sure you are," Logan murmurs. "You just died, Fantome."

I send him a glare to silence him. That's all I need—all Mama needs—is for word to get out I died and Logan Cross saved me.

"Is she okay?" a woman's voice calls. I don't look toward the fence, but recognize it all the same. Prissy Barnes, my nemesis.

"All I need is to check on Tabitha." I ignore her and point toward the house for Logan's benefit. "And take something for my pounding head."

"I'll take care of the cat," Logan assures me. "She and Mox get along just fine, don't you Mox?" He pats the dog's head, and they move away to let Stout and his partner, a young kid named Wesley, wrestle me up onto the gurney. "You go to the clinic and let Doc check you out."

Everyone is insisting on this, including the police officer— one who used to work under my father, before Mama insisted he quit the force and sent him off to pursue his dream of being a rock singer. If I weren't still hearing the cats—including the door knocker—continuing to discuss my clumsiness and the fact Aunt Willa's killer is near, I'd refuse.

Killer...?

I push Wesley out of the way and look at the gargoyle cats. Then at the gathering crowd. Most of the faces are familiar...I can't believe any of them would hurt my aunt.

Since last night, I've felt, heard, and seen things that I haven't since I was a girl. And the more I hear these voices in my head, the more fearful I become of the truth. Did Mama truly overhear Aunt Willa arguing with someone last night? Did that someone contribute to her death?

"Ava?" another woman's voice calls. "Do you want me to call your mother?"

This one sounds familiar, but I can't place her face when I meet her eyes. "No," I call back. "I'm fine!"

A firm hand lands on my shoulder, and I glance at the owner, Reverend Stout, who stares me down with the righteousness only a preacher or Sunday school teacher can deliver adequately. "Ava, dear. You are going to the clinic."

My eyes swim and the memory of Aunt Willa in the mist rushes over me.

If I'm seeing ghosts and hearing inanimate objects speak, maybe I *do* need my head examined.

"You'll need a key, Logan. I'm sure Tabitha is safe and sound inside, but we need to check."

He motions for me to lie down. "Got one. Don't worry."

How does he have a key to my aunt's house? The pounding in my head is too much now, and the lightheadedness is returning with a vengeance. With Wesley and the Rev's help, I ease down onto the gurney. "My cats..." I point in the direction of my car. "They're inside."

Logan pats my leg. "Ava, I've got it. I promise to take good care of them."

All three gargoyles snort.

Chapter Five

❦

Two hours later, I check myself out of the tiny, medicinal-smelling Sacred Heart clinic, against Dr. Abernathy's advice.

The aging, but still handsome, physician in his white coat and round spectacles declared I have a concussion but could find no reason for my near-death experience. I'm breathing fine, all the equipment shows my heart rate and pulse are normal, and, in fact, I'm in good shape.

Doc is old school and wants to dig deeper into my brain, but he doesn't possess the equipment for an MRI and I'm not driving twenty miles east for a scan at the nearest large hospital. I hit my head, blacked out, and maybe stopped breathing for a minute. No big deal.

We have a long discussion about my aunt, who I suspect he had a soft spot for, and his sympathies over her death nearly reduce me to tears. I swear I see the glimmer of them in his eyes as well. He's a widower who moved to town five or six years ago, and from what Mama's told me he has quite a fan club with the local widows. His compassion for others is obvious.

Finally, with an official white paper listing his diagnosis and referral to a trauma specialist in Macon, I walk out into the murky sunlight and realize I don't have my car.

At least my head feels mildly better. If only I had something for my empty stomach and some coffee. My stomach has settled, but last night's cold pizza is long gone.

Shading my eyes with one hand, I scan the street, mentally counting the blocks to Aunt Willa's. Sixteen, if memory serves.

In my pj's and dirty robe, with the remnants of my concussion still causing a slight bit of vertigo, I start off for the edge of the parking lot.

Doc's nurse called Mama earlier and got no answer. No surprise, since she took a sleeping pill before I got her into bed. The nurse, a woman who's as old as the outdated *National Geographic* magazines in Doc's waiting room, then called my mother's best friend, Queenie, who went to check on her. While Doc was arguing with me about the brain scan, Queenie reported back that Mama was sleeping like a baby.

Thornhollow doesn't have taxis, and I'm reluctant to call any of my friends. I know pretty much everyone in town, but I've never been good at asking for help. Besides, I need a moment alone to try and figure out everything that's happened since last night. I probably should turn around and go back into the clinic and have Doc write me a prescription to see a psychiatrist.

My clogs clunk on the sidewalk as I head east, a cheery sign at the side of the road telling me I'm entering historic downtown Thornhollow in three more blocks.

As I walk, the night's events replay in my mind. Being adept at suppressing weird experiences, I successfully convince myself that stress caused me to believe the door knocker and gargoyles were talking to me. The fresh air and the weak October sunlight seem to confirm that for the next block, and I actually pick up my speed a bit.

Aunt Willa's ghost, however? That's another story.

Wilhelmina Rae Holloway Duchamp was a psychic medium.

She used to encourage my own psychic gifts, and until I was seven years old I often couldn't tell the difference between the living and the dead who walked the streets of our town.

A frightening experience with an earthbound ghost caused me to shut down my "gift"—if gift is the right term for it. This pleased my parents, who didn't want the town to realize their daughter was a fruit loop but disappointed my aunt considerably. While she kept her own abilities under wraps, mostly for my mother's sake, she continued to show me ways to psychically protect myself.

"Maybe I was just hallucinating," I say out loud as I walk. "Mama's anxiety planted a seed of fear in my brain, and the concussion turned it into a dream."

You died, the voice in my head argues. *Stop denying it.*

The trees lining the street form a canopy and birds sing overhead. The air is warming up, last night's frost gone.

Even now, the details are fuzzy. Aunt Willa's words float through my mind, unbidden. There was something about my bedroom in her house and a trunk.

Still, dream or not, I wonder if my subconscious is confirming the fact she was murdered.

No, I argue with myself. I must have latched onto that suspicion because of Mama claiming to have heard her sister arguing with someone.

A sleek vintage red Porsche pulls up alongside me. The convertible top is down, and a sad-eyed basset sits in the back seat. Logan Cross smiles at me from behind the wheel and a pair of aviator sunglasses. "Need a ride, Fantome?"

I keep walking and he cruises slowly alongside. I debate getting in the car, although I certainly could use a ride. Maybe because he and his family have always been in the upper echelon of Thornhollow, while my mine has been on the opposite side. Even though my mother is mayor, we are working-class people.

"I brought coffee." He taps the white lid of a travel cup. "Queenie sent her famous pumpkin muffins. Said that would help your broken heart. We thought you'd still be in a hospital bed."

"Checked myself out. I'm good to go, and Mama's gonna need me today."

He holds up the white bag, the car still creeping along beside me. My stomach growls and I nearly falter, thinking about Queenie's muffins.

"She'll be by after the morning rush with a pot of chicken and dumplings for you and your mother," Logan continues.

Food, the Southern equivalent of love. Queenie LaFleur, owner of the Beehive Diner, is the best cook in three counties, if not the whole state. My stomach makes itself known again and my bloodstream craves the coffee and sugar. It's everything I can do not to lick my lips.

Logan puts the bag in the passenger seat. "You're staying through the weekend, right?"

I haven't even considered what's next. A funeral, the insurance paperwork, who'll take over the wedding business... There's suddenly a lot to consider. My knee-jerk reaction is a standard for me though. "I have to get back to Atlanta as soon as possible. My job, you know."

Those blue eyes narrow. "Surely, you can take a week off. Willa Rae was supposed to lead the parade Friday night, and she always heads up the Main Street trick-or-treat party come Halloween. Saturday is the Burnett-Durham wedding at the country club. Miranda is no doubt freaking out since Willa Rae was in charge of it. And Sunday is the Pumpkin and Peaches Wine Tour. Your aunt is—*was*—working with my folks for our part of it."

His mother must be freaking out as much as Miranda Burnett over her poor wedding.

Maybe I do have a concussion, because I feel overwhelmed

at the thought of sorting through all those events. "Why was Aunt Willa leading the parade? I thought the president of the chamber of commerce did that."

"Ava, she is—*was*, sorry—the president."

Wow, she didn't tell me. I definitely need that coffee. "Look, she just died last night. I need time to wrap my head around everything. I'm sure Mama and Rosie will get all that stuff figured out."

"I'm sure they will." He glances down the street, back to me. "Are you seriously going to walk all the way to The Wedding Chapel?"

"Are my cats okay?"

"Safe and sound at my place."

I wonder what his place looks like. He lives in the space above his law office, if I recall. "And Tabby?" I wonder what we're going to do with her. Mama's never cared for pets. "Is she okay? Did you feed her?"

He grips the steering wheel a little tighter. "Yeah, about that..."

I stop walking. "What?"

He eases the car to a stop. "I searched the house and the grounds. I couldn't find her."

"What do you mean, you couldn't find her? Where is she?"

He shrugs. "Willa Rae never let her out, but I looked everywhere. No cat."

I open the car door, grab the white bag and slide in. "Well, don't just sit there." I open the travel cup and down some coffee. "Step on it."

Chapter Six

✦❧✦

Main Street is hopping with people and it isn't even 9
a.m. when most of the shops open. Tourists and
townspeople alike are filtering in for the fall
festival.

Everyone knows Logan and they wave as we go by, the
canopy of trees lining the street causing shadows to flicker
over us.

As we pull up to Aunt Willa's house, I see two vehicles at the
curb. From one jumps a curvy blonde with big hair, dressed in
an expensive tweed coat, who hauls a stack of books from her
backseat.

From the second vehicle further down emerges raven-haired
Priscilla Barnes, owner of Boss Lady Events, and the only
serious competition my aunt had within three counties. Priscilla
is carrying a casserole in hand.

"This looks like fun," Logan says, and I send him a
besmirching glare.

Prissy Barnes and I are longtime enemies. She's been
needling herself into my life since she pushed me off the
bleachers in eighth grade, breaking my leg and ruining my

already slim chances of making the cheerleading squad. Revenge came in the form of me stealing her boyfriend, Charles Caldwell II, from her, right before junior prom.

Aunt Willa always said she was jealous of me, but I never could figure out why. She was rich, popular, and seemed happy. Why would she be jealous of me?

Logan shifts into park and turns off the motor. He looks as though he might pull out a bag of popcorn and sit back to watch the show. Moxley, head between us, drools on my arm.

"What are you doing?" I grab the bakery bag with the muffin and try to ignore the growing headache at the back of my skull.

"Getting ready for the fireworks." He leans close and lowers his voice, "Heads up, in case Willa didn't mention it, Priscilla has been trying to sabotage her business for the past year."

Tell me something I don't know.

Priscilla spots us and waves. She's waving at Logon of course, not me. The former prom queen of Thornhollow High School is in the same league as the man sitting next to me. "I'm cancelling the show," I tell him with a fake smile. "You'll have to get your jollies elsewhere."

He gives Prissy a return wave and smiles warmly at her. Without thought, I reach out and smack his arm.

"What's that for?" he asks indignantly.

Silly me, I thought he was on my side. "Fraternizing with the enemy."

The blonde fidgets from one foot to the other on the sidewalk as I get out of the car. She's practically humming with tension. "Ava, I am so sorry about Miss Willa! And I hate to intrude, but..."

I pass by her to open the gate, scanning for Tabitha. The cat never goes outside, even though she has a cat door. She has to be in the house, I tell myself, probably hiding after all of the commotion. A little kibble or canned tuna should coax her out.

"Ava?" The blonde is on my heels. "You *are* going to take over for Miss Willa, right? You're going to handle my wedding?"

Ah, this must be Miranda Burnett. I haven't laid eyes on her in years, and she looks like her mother, now that I really look at her. Especially with that 'do.

Priscilla's chatting with Logan at the car. There's lots of smiling, her hand grazing his arm. He steps around her, reaching to lift Moxley out, and the two of them stroll to the open gate.

The poor bride-to-be shifts into my line of vision and the sheer magnitude of her hair makes my head pound harder. She has clips and bobby pins with pearls all over it tugging each strand and pearl into a perfect coif.

"Let me guess, you've been to the salon?" I ask, pointing at her hair.

One hand touches a curl. "Deciding on my wedding look." Her soft accent accentuates her worries. "Princess did it before her first appointment this morning. I was going to do half up, half down, but I don't know. All up? All down? I can't decide. I was going to ask Miss...your aunt."

Princess is Queenie's sister. She runs the Beehive Hair Salon a block over.

"What about leaving it natural?" I offer. It looks to be long. "Some soft curls on the end would be nice."

She looks at me with serious darks eyes, "Ava, you do know who I am, right?"

Priscilla, Logan, and Moxley reach us. Priscilla steps up and grabs the woman by the arm. "Don't you worry, Miranda. I'll be happy to take over your wedding."

"Of course I know who you are, Miranda. You're marrying Ty Durham, heir to the DH candy empire."

Priscilla steers Miranda around, holding out the casserole to me with her other hand. The 9x13 glass is covered with foil. "Sorry about Willa," she says, offhandedly, but she's hiding a smile. Probably because she's stealing one of Willa's biggest customers this year. To Miranda, she says, "Avalon doesn't know much about weddings, having never had one herself."

Mama raised me to be polite and respectful to all people, but she also raised me to stand up to bullies.

Ignoring the casserole, I grab Miranda's other arm, the one holding the books and brides magazines. "Miss Burnett, you know you're in good hands with me. Willa taught me everything I know, and I've dressed nearly two hundred brides, including the mayor of Atlanta's daughter. I even helped our beloved governor's niece in my time as head bridal consultant at Southern Bridal Flair in Atlanta. Plus, as I mentioned, Willa had a good influence on me. I spent my teenage years working for her at every event she coordinated."

I flash the ladylike smile Mama ingrained in me for the campaign trail from the time I was four and lean toward Prissy, lowering my voice like I'm trying to keep this between us, when really I'm not. "You know, last time I heard, being married three times hasn't helped your business in the least. Makes me wonder if you're jinxed."

Miranda gasps, pulling her arm from Priscilla's hand. Over Prissy's shoulder, Logan smothers a laugh.

An older red Celica draws up to the curb. Rosie Rodriguez hops out, big hair, even bigger attitude, and a handbag the size of Texas.

"Come on, Miss Burnett." Miranda moves closer to me. "Let's go over the details together inside."

Prissy raises her nose in the air and looks down at us. "You'll regret this." I'm not sure if she's talking to me or Miranda. "She'll screw this up like she does everything else, I guarantee it."

Okay, must be Miranda. But the criticism is meant to cut me. Prissy turns on her heel and whizzes by Logan in a hasty retreat with her nose in the air. He gives a small wave goodbye but she ignores him.

Maribelle Rosie Rodriquez, my aunt's right-hand assistant, hustles by her, nearly knocking her off the path, the giant bag slung over one shoulder. A tiny chihuahua head peaks out the top as she nods at Logan then looks genuinely alarmed at my appearance. "Ava, I didn't realize you would be opening up The Chapel today." She manages to hug me, her ample bosom squishing up between us. The dog sucks its head inside the tote. "Blessed Mother, you should be with your mama."

"She's sleeping," I offer, "and Miranda needs reassurances about her wedding."

Even in her three-inch heels Rosie's barely my height. A heavy gold cross lies on her collarbone. "I'm just devastated about Miss Willa. Is there anything I can do for you or Miss Della?"

"Mama and I have a lot to figure out," I admit, shooting a sideways glance at our nervous bride. "Can you take Miss Burnett inside and get her some coffee? I need to look for Tabby. She's missing."

Her hand goes to the handbag. "Oh dear!"

Miranda looks around, as if searching for the cat. "Do you want us to help you look?"

I lay a hand on her arm. "Thank you. I appreciate that, but I'll handle it. You go in with Rosie and make sure all the details for the wedding are in order, okay?"

Rosie gives Miranda a full smile and ushers her up the steps. "Are you excited?" she asks the bride, glancing over her shoulder at me and winking to let me know everything is handled. The two disappear inside as Priscilla peels off from the curb.

Logan and I watch. "Nicely done," he says to me, reaching down to scratch Moxley between the ears. The two head for the steps.

"Where do you think you're going?" I block them, noticing the apple I tripped over earlier is back in its place on the display.

"To look for Tabitha," he says as if it isn't obvious.

"I appreciate your reviving me after my fall and giving me a ride home from the clinic, but I'll take it from here. Thanks."

"I save your life and that's the thanks I get?" There's a sparkle in his eyes. He lifts Moxley up, brushing past me, to get to the top. "I'll go get your cats and bring them over. Then I'll help find Tabby."

My cats! Poor babies. I've nearly forgotten about them in the melee.

I stare down at Moxley. "Come on, then." I step onto the porch, the eyes of the gargoyle cats following me as Logan heads for his place across the street. "Don't you dare say a word," I mutter to them.

"What was that?" Logan calls.

"Nothing," I yell over my shoulder, holding the door for the waddling dog.

Thankfully, the gargoyles remain silent.

Chapter Seven

☙❦❧

My aunt's house smells like roses and her floral perfume. There are always fresh roses because her friend, Betty Lee, the town florist, brings a dozen every week for Aunt Willa's desk. In turn, Willa promoted Betty's services.

The front entryway, with rooms to the left and right, were long ago remodeled into one large open space. Each room showcases a large display window, and Rosie's desk is on the right.

Behind her, a fireplace, once anchoring the formal living room, is surrounded by bookshelves. Arranged in front is a couch and chairs with a coffee table between them piled with assorted bridal books and magazines, offering a comfortable space to work with clients.

At the far end is an old grandfather clock that bongs with a deep baritone as I study this home away from home.

To the left are double doors that open into Aunt Willa's office. Stacks of binders filled with dresses, tuxedoes, and other wedding essentials are piled high on a nearby credenza. Her grand desk has no computer, but rather pictures of the family and a large calendar with all of her upcoming events listed in her bold handwriting. There are assorted tables with books and binders, posters of upcoming town events, and samples of wedding cakes, invitations and décor.

As Rosie talks Miranda off the wedding disaster cliff, I make my way to the kitchen. Moxley follows, his own waddling pace a match to mine. I might as well make the coffee since Rosie and her dog aren't going to get a break from our client anytime soon.

As I slip into the lemony-scented space, Moxley, nose to the ground, disappears toward the back of the house. Sipping what's left of Queenie's coffee from the travel mug, I pull out the ancient coffee pot and get it brewing.

As it heats water, I cut my muffin into quarters, lean against the countertop near the sink, and try to gather my thoughts. Aunt Willa's garden boots sit in the mudroom, off the kitchen, under her raincoat and assorted sun hats. I barely taste the muffin as I see a memory of her bustling around, washing herbs she's picked from her garden, filling the tea kettle, laughing about a joke. My gaze trails to the window next to the ailing fridge and scans the part of the backyard I can see.

The sugar and caffeine hit my blood stream a moment later, and I feel moderately calmer. Aunt Willa's cup from the previous day still sits on the kitchen table, as if she were coming back for it.

The shock of her death hits me all over again, and along with the lack of sleep and my mild concussion, I feel a bout of anxiety. Once I find Tabitha, I'll change clothes, check on Mama, and will make plans for the business, the house, the cat.

But right now, all I want to do is wash out Aunt Willa's coffee cup and pretend that she's going to rush into the kitchen at any moment, her face lighting up at seeing me.

The squeak of the front door alerts me to Logan's return. The reunion with my cats is precious, both letting me know they are happy to see me and equally unhappy they haven't yet had breakfast.

"Thanks again for taking care of them," I tell him. "Can I offer you coffee?"

He goes to a cabinet and pulls out a mug, as if he's at home here. "Happy to oblige. Any sign of Tabitha?"

I ignore the irritation at his helping himself, taking out two serving size cans of cat food from the pantry. "Not a peep," I tell Logan.

Scooping some salmon and rice combo onto dessert plates, I call the missing cat. Arthur and Lancelot inhale their servings but Tabby doesn't appear. Logan and I both call her again.

"Bring the food," he says. "We'll find her."

He pours an extra cup of coffee and takes it to Miranda, who blushes and thanks him repeatedly. He offers to get Rosie a cup, and I swear her cheeks raise a flush as well, even though she shakes her head no.

As I prowl through the den, guest bathroom, and laundry on the first floor, a host of memories assail me, but the cat does not appear. By the time I reach the grand staircase, Logan joins me, as does his dog.

"How's your head?" he asks.

"Still hurts," I grumble, "but I'm fine."

He shoots me a wry grin. "Of course, you are. You've got that Fantome hard head, I imagine."

I wave the open can of smelly food around, hoping the fancy salmon mixture will cajole the cat from her hiding spot. My cats entangle themselves under my feet, hoping they'll get a second helping.

The railing of the dark, highly polished staircase is wound with fall garland. The upstairs consists of three bedrooms, a large bath, and a sitting area. There are more steps to the walk-up attic. I hesitate outside Aunt Willa's room, the worn wool carpet runner scratchy under my feet. "Why do you have a key to this place?" I ask Logan again.

He leans on the wall across from me, sipping his coffee. "Why don't you come over to the office later and I'll explain everything?" He points downward, indicating Rosie and Miranda. "Now probably isn't the best time."

A nervous flutter in my stomach makes me wish I hadn't downed as much coffee as I did. Annoyed at his non-answer, I step inside the bedroom, check under the bed, in the closet, and avoid the armoire, the memory of my aunt's voice ringing in my head. Logan moves to the door frame, watching me with his intelligent eyes.

"I'm going back to Atlanta this afternoon, after Mama and I figure a few things out." This announcement actually surprises me, but it seems logical and I refuse to admit Logan flusters me a little. "I need to call my boss, set up a few days' of personal leave for the funeral, and..."

I trail off, trying to come up with more reasons to get out of town and back to my comfort zone. I'm afraid it's the only way I'll be able to think through all of this. "I need clothes," I add to the list. "For the funeral."

Brilliant. I sound like an idiot.

Logan nods, as if this makes perfect sense, and I'm slightly relieved. And then he says, "I'm sure Edith has black dresses your size at her shop. Can't you call your boss from here?"

Of course, he would have to be practical. Edith Warhol certainly has black dresses at her clothing store. Plain, boring, perfect dresses for Aunt Willa's funeral.

Except, I don't think my aunt would want that. She was such a bright personality, I believe she would be happier in heaven if all of us sang and danced at her funeral. We should wear bright clothes, reflecting the type of woman she was while she was here.

Funerals in Thornhollow are taken very seriously, and every

woman in town knows part of her community standing revolves around the food she brings to the wake and the outfit she wears to the funeral.

I brush past Logan at the door and walk toward the second bedroom—mine. I spent lots of nights here with Aunt Willa, most of my summers, too.

Inside, Moxley is lying beside the giant cedar chest against the far wall. "Here, Tabby," I call and then to Logan, "I have a life in Atlanta, responsibilities."

Arthur and Lancelot jump on the bed, meowing loudly at me. They are still hoping for more food. Tabby doesn't show and I eye the chest, as Logan checks the closet.

"Of course, I just thought…" Accusation weights his tone with the unsaid words.

I see my old sketch pad on the nightstand. Another in the bay window. Dresses. I used to love to sketch wedding dresses, always trying to create my dream one. "Thought what, Logan?"

"I was under the impression Willa Ray was turning over the business to you—she mentioned you were coming home to take over. Since you've been here, all you've done is insist you're not moving home."

The letter flashes through my mind. I look out the window, shifting the lace curtain aside. So many memories, this house, my beloved aunt. They all encompass the word *home* to me.

Protect the family, her letter had said. *Protect the town*. What did she mean?

Before I can respond to tell him I can't move home and take over her business, I see a streak of orange below in the garden.

"It's Tabby," I say, and jet out the bedroom door.

Chapter Eight

I fly out the back door, and the screen door slams against the house as I race down the steps. "Tabby!"

The backyard is nearly two acres of rolling lawn, maple, oak, and birch trees, a white arch covered in ivy and jasmine vines spotlighted on my right.

Logan emerges behind me. He comes to my side on the path as I scan for that streak of orange. "Where did you see her?"

"Over there." I point toward the fountain on the left, a three-tiered white concrete goddess with a flowing watery moat that people often throw money in to make wishes. A paper birch stands nearby, the yellow and rust-colored leaves filling the water and carpeting the ground. "But she was headed that way."

Another point, this time in the other direction. Moxley ambles down the back steps, his short legs carrying him past us, so he can sniff an azalea bush that still holds onto a few weepy blooms.

"I'll take this side," Logan says, motioning toward the fountain. "You take that one."

The path leads past the arch of ivy. "Tabitha," I call, waving the open can around to distribute the scent. "Here, Tabby."

Moxley trails across the stone path, nose to the ground, his floppy ears dragging on the wet grass. The humidity is high, the sun gaining strength.

A red maple leaf flutters to the ground at my feet. The tree is probably a hundred years old, and still holding on to the majority of its leaves. As the dog and I wind along the path, a host of burning bushes, like small fires in amongst the boxwood and poplars, offset the lingering mist.

Where would I hide if I were a cat? I think.

"Certainly not under wet bushes," I mutter to myself. I check around the benches under the arch and a ledge built up with stones, where people often sit for their engagement or wedding pictures. My aunt loves to hold engagement parties and small weddings back here.

There's a gazebo further down the hill, and I check that, too, hoping to find the cat sitting high and dry.

As the landscape slopes, my shoes slide on the wet leaves. Tabby is nowhere to be found, and the creek bed bubbles in the distance, the fresh rain forcing it to nearly overflow its low banks.

A mockingbird calls to me from the willow near the creek, the long sweeping branches of the tree swaying to and fro in the breeze. While the temperature is rising, I feel a chill. The scent of damp moss and leaves tickles my nose as I grow closer.

The old Holloway homestead stands like a sentry off to the southwest, looking as sad as the willow. Its structure of ancient stones and timber having withstood hundreds of years but are now shabby and falling apart.

How I wish those stones could talk. Not only would it tell of the founders of Thornhollow—my very distant ancestor, Tabitha Holloway having lived here—but it might also tell me what happened to my poor aunt.

In my mind, I see Aunt Willa standing by the creek. She loved it here, and often came to this spot to do her own form of meditation. Said the running water and beautiful trees helped her think when life got hard. I spent many a summer down here playing in the creek myself. There was a time when together we built fairy houses and held luncheons here.

I think back to Mama and her claim that Aunt Willa was arguing with someone. Looking around, my chest tightens, my breathing becomes labored. It's as if I'm having the same heart attack as my aunt, even though I realize it's only grief invading my chest.

I rub the center of my rib cage and feel my eyes sting with tears. I haven't allowed myself a proper cry, but there's no time for it now. I keep expecting to hear Willa call my name, to see her run out of the house and down to the creek. I wish I could feel her arms wrap around me one more time.

Moxley, who I left back at the gazebo, ambles to the bank, his ears dark with moisture. He noses around at the edge, sticking his face in the water. Afraid the dog will fall in—can basset hounds swim?—I call to him to get back.

He steps closer. Water rushes over his fat paws and his snout.

"Dumb dog," I mutter.

The creek seems wild today, untamed. "Moxley," I chastise, "get back here."

Nose down, he ignores me and takes yet another step, water now nearly to his low-hanging chest.

Mine grows tighter, my fingers cold with a sudden numbness. Mist rises from the water and slips between the trees on the other side of the bank, weaving its way toward us.

A shadow moves in that fog and I squint, moving toward the dog. A deer, I tell myself. They are plentiful this time of year.

I reach Moxley and tug on his collar. He must weight fifty pounds, maybe more, and he doesn't budge.

I scold him again, as creek water splashes on both of us.

"Come on," I urge. "The last thing I need is for you to end up drowning."

The dog raises his nose and sniffs the air. Without warning, he lets out a howl. The sad note sends a chill over my already cold skin and echoes through the trees.

The mockingbird flies away, the last of the cry dying amongst the leaves. Across the expanse, the shadow in the woods disappears, too. In my body, I feel the sound of the dog's bellow, as if it expressed my grief.

Moxley looks at me and then back to the water.

"Cut me some slack, here," I say to him, sighing. "You fall in, and your owner will never forgive me."

The drooping, bloodshot eyes rise to mine again. He turns his stocky body slowly around and heads back toward the garden.

"Dumb human."

"What?" I twist around to watch his progress as he lumbers off. My focus shifts to the ground, my pulse ricocheting. "No, no, no," I whisper to myself. "Not again."

The leaves overhead shift and sunlight breaks through. A sparkle in the water around the rocks catches my eye.

"Hey." Logan jogs up to me as I bend down and reach for the sparkling item. "I heard Moxley howl. Everything okay?"

Lifting the object from the water, my throat feels closed off. The gold chain is broken, the antique key that used to hang from it gone.

"Is that…?" Logan moves closer, his shoulder brushing mine as he eyes it.

Still kneeling, I clutch the chain and scan the creek bed for the key, the rushing water making it difficult to see. "Yes. Aunt Willa's favorite necklace."

He must know what I'm searching for and scans the water up and down the bank, but we see nothing of the key. He helps me stand, his warm hand reassuring on my cold one.

He leads me a few feet away from the rushing water. "I didn't see the cat," he said.

The chain is as cold as my fingers. Numbly, I try to process what happened. "I'll keep looking for her."

His phone rings, the modern sound out of place here in this ancient environment.

"Yes, Norman." He walks off a few yards to have his conversation. "No, I didn't forget. I'll be there in a minute. I'm just across the street."

He returns, pocketing the phone a moment later. "Sorry," he says. "Morning appointment I'll come back as soon as I can."

All I do is nod, an empty feeling in my chest, as he heads for the back porch. Moxley falls into step behind him.

I pocket the broken chain and start that way myself, my body tired and weary, when movement to my left makes me turn.

As I glance toward the old homestead, I do a double-take.

A naked woman is ducking inside.

Chapter Nine

❦

This is the weirdest day ever.

Well, it's right up there anyway. Last December, I helped my friends, the Whitethorne sisters, save the world from an evil entity, and it's hard to compete with that, but today ranks right up there with it.

Brambles and overgrowth thwart my progress to the Holloway house, once a landmark, now forgotten. Samuel Thornton and Tabitha Holloway built it and lived here when they founded this town. An unheard of thing back in the late 1700s, an unmarried couple, kicked out of Colonial Virginia under suspicious circumstances and ending up here, combining their last names to give birth to a new place.

The wooden door, gray with age, is slightly ajar and hanging crookedly from its hinges. Prickly blackberry vines create a canopy over the doorway and around the single stone step. Ivy creeps over the outside walls, and as I push the door farther open, the scent of mold and decay hits my nose.

Several degrees colder in here than outside, the forest has been trying to reclaim the farmhouse for as long as I can remember.

Aunt Willa always talked of restoring it, creating a landmark once more, but she never seemed to have the time or money.

"Hello?" I call. "Are you okay? I saw you outside."

The interior is shadowy and dark, dank from the previous night's rain. A broken window on the north wall has let rain leak in, along with several cracks in the ceiling.

Critters have been in here, leaving droppings and nests. This is the last place I want to be, but I must find the woman I just spotted and figure out what she's doing here.

Could she be the person Aunt Willa was arguing with?

Surely no one, not even a vagrant, would take up residence in this dilapidated place. I wonder if the woman is hurt, or perhaps mentally ill. Whoever she is, she can't stay.

"My name's Ava. If you need help, I'll get it for you." I make my way past what was once a kitchen, a cavernous fireplace still intact with a large black iron pot hanging over ashes.

The only sound I hear is a constant drip from the corner of the ceiling. I look for signs that someone's been squatting here and see none. Apparently, only the forest creatures have made this their home.

"Hello," I call again. "Did you know my aunt?"

Did you kill her? I think, and stop walking, the idea triggering a flicker of fear low in my stomach.

I debate whether to continue the hunt or to simply call the police and ask them to come check it out.

Shoring up my nerves—because she could be a killer, and because there could be mice and other rodents—I go deeper into the dim interior. My legs shake, mostly because I don't do mice any more than I do confronting a potential murderer.

Especially one running around in her birthday suit.

My nerves get the better of me and I turn to leave. I'll call the police. Before I can take a step toward the open door, however, something crashes to the floor beyond the living room.

I stop in my tracks. If this girl didn't kill my aunt, she still could be a witness. That thought gets me moving toward the hall. I see a semi-closed door off to the side. A shadow shifts behind it.

Gotcha. "Look," I say using my most reasonable voice—the one I use on hysterical brides when necessary—"if you're in trouble, talk to me. I'll do whatever I can to help. Otherwise, I'm going to call the police. You're trespassing, and it's quite dangerous to even be in here. You'll have to explain to them what you're doing."

I hear a low chuckle from the other side of the door. "You dunnah want to do that young Ava," a soft, very Scottish sounding woman's voice says.

Goosebumps run over my skin and I take a step back.

At least I've got her talking to me. Removing my robe, I force my shaky legs to the doorway. I hand the robe through the opening. "Here, take this to cover yourself. Then come out here and tell me who you are and why your trespassing."

"Trespassing?" She's indignant.

There's a bright flash—bright enough that it makes me flinch back. A high-pitched screech like someone stepped on the tail of a cat echoes through the room and out into the hall.

Suddenly, Tabby—the cat—bolts through the space between my feet, startling me so bad I jump and trip, trying not to step on her. I manage to fall into a reed chair nearby and it breaks into pieces when we both hit the floor.

Adrenaline pumps through my veins, and I scramble back to my feet. "Wait, Tabby!"

I follow her, now covered in dirt. My hand lands in cobwebs, and I shake it trying to get rid of them. I tuck the robe under my arm as I hustle through the living room once more.

Tabitha stands on her four paws in the open doorway, whiskers twitching. She sniffs the air and meows. "Find the key." She glances over her feline shoulder at me. "He took it."

Oh lord. The cat is talking to me. Worse, it has the Scottish brogue of the naked woman. "Who?" I dare to ask, wondering at my sanity.

"Ava?" Rosie's voice interrupts, sounding distant as it echoes down the rolling hill and plays tag amongst the trees. "Where are you?"

Tabby flicks her marmalade-striped tail. "Find the key and you'll find the killer."

A final flick, and she's gone.

Chapter Ten

As I step out of the house, a booming male voice ripples through the air. "Avalon Fantome!"

A giant of a black man stands in the sun, his bald head shining. His purple velvet vest, topped off with a flamboyant silver scarf, makes me smile.

"Braxton?"

Long legs eat up the ground, carrying him to meet me. "What in the Sam Hill are you doing in that old place?" he asks, but he's smiling and I throw myself into his outstretched arms.

It's like being wrapped in steel. Braxton LaFleur is the closest thing to an older brother I've ever had. He smells like black coffee, pumpkin muffins, and clean aftershave.

His embrace is just what I need, and he lifts me off the ground, swinging me around like I'm a little girl. "You've been in town nine hours and didn't so much as text me?" He sets me down, his face as indignant as his voice. "You should be ashamed."

Yes, I should. "Things have been a mess. My phone died on the way here and I haven't recharged it."

His dark eyes convey hurt. "You could have had the clinic call me to pick you up this morning."

"During rush hour at the Honey Bar?" The son of Queenie, he's a true businessman. His place is a coffee bar by morning and a liquor establishment once 4 p.m. comes around. It's located next to his mama's restaurant.

He throws his head back and laughs. "In case you've forgotten, I'm the owner and I do have minions who can hold down the fort for me, y'know? Where's that phone? We need to get it recharged ASAP."

I smile. "In my car." We walk the stone path toward the house, passing the gazebo side by side, and thoughts about talking cats and my aunt's weird demise leave for a brief moment or two. "Did you happen to see Tabby jet by you?" I ask him.

"What's she doing out here?" Brax scans the area, searching for her. "Did you let her out of the house?"

Rosie is waiting on the screened in porch, looking anxious. She gives me a little wave, as if wanting me to hurry.

"I guess she escaped last night," I tell Brax. "I don't know what happened to her. Or Aunt Willa," I add.

He drops a muscled arm around my shoulder. "Honey, your auntie lived a good life. This town was her everything and it will be tough to fill her shoes, but right now, the ladies auxiliary has descended, and we need to get you cleaned up. I'll come back out and look for the cat, but honey, you're a fright."

No wonder Rosie looks anxious. As we climb the back steps, she holds the screen door open for us. I look back over my shoulder one last time. "I need to find Tabitha." And I do, but it's also a reason to avoid the ladies auxiliary.

In my pocket, the chain has warmed, and I grab hold of it like a lifeline. I pull it out and hold it up in the sunlight filtering through the screen to examine it. I can see where the chain broke in two. "And I need to find the key. It's missing."

Brax and Rosie exchange a look. They know what I'm talking about. "Well, it surely isn't in that old homestead," Brax says with a shudder. "That place is haunted, Ava, and the ghosts can have it if it's in there."

Ghosts—is that what I saw? The naked woman seemed real enough, and Tabitha had the same voice. Was the woman a ghost who took over poor Tabby's form?

A new idea hits and it's so preposterous I take a step back. Is Tabitha…?

"Ava?" Rosie snaps me out of my thoughts, her finger caressing one end of the chain still dangling in the air. "Where did you find this?"

"The creek. It must have broken when she fell in. *If* she fell in."

Brax's thick eyebrows draw together in confusion. "What do you mean *if*? Sorry to be crass, but they found her face down in the water, didn't they? "

"Mama thinks she heard Aunt Willa arguing with someone right before she died. What if they knocked her into it, choked her, and drowned her?"

Rosie looks dismayed. "That's a horrible thing to say."

Brax grabs me by both shoulders. "Your auntie had a heart attack, honey. Then she fell into the creek."

They're both looking at me like I've lost my mind. That's not out of the question, I guess.

Tabitha's words ring in my ears. *He killed her.*

I'm not sure there's anyone in the world who knows me better than Braxton. I almost confess all, telling him about Tabitha talking, the inanimate objects out front as well. They all insist Aunt Willa was killed, murdered.

I'm starting to think the same thing, but why? Who in the world would hurt my poor aunt?

Behind us, deeper inside the house, I hear the rise and fall of female voices and laughter. It brings me back to reality, and I shake off the idea of confessing to Braxton and Rosie what's been going on in my head. "Why are they here?" I whisper. "Why didn't they go to Mama's house?"

Brax releases my shoulders. He's still looking at me as though he's worried about my health. "They tried. Your mother wouldn't let them in. Said she was going to work, if you can believe that."

I believe it. I guess the sleep meds wore off. And not even those or her sister's death will keep Mama from her office. It's a coping mechanism. We're both well versed in it.

"What should I do with all the food?" Rosie asks. "The fridge is already full."

Brax takes the lead, guiding us into the mudroom. "First, Ava needs a shower and makeup," he says. "I'll handle the food and get that cell phone charged. Then the auxiliary."

We continue into the kitchen and he lowers his voice. "After that, we'll find Tabby, the key, and get you and Mama Della to the funeral parlor to make the proper arrangements."

I'm chilled to the bone all over again, my mind swimming with responsibilities and the idea my aunt may have been murdered. At the mention of the funeral parlor, my stomach clenches. I need answers and haven't a clue where to look for them. "I think I'm losing my mind," I say under my breath.

"You're shaking like a leaf." Brax rubs one of my arms. "Let's get you in a hot shower." He pushes me toward the back stairs, and over his shoulder he calls to Rosie, "Take the overflow food next door to Uphill's. He has that huge commercial fridge for the B&B. Plus, he won't mind snitching some of it for himself and his very full guest list this weekend."

Rosie looks relieved. "I'm on it."

Twenty minutes later, I'm showered and Brax has blown out my hair and applied generous amounts of makeup. I'm still eight hours short on sleep, but like any proper Southern lady I'm hiding it under a smile and extra concealer.

"Ready?" Brax holds out a hand to me on the stairs.

Slipping mine into his, I draw a deep breath. The ladies auxiliary will be my undoing if I'm not careful, but after the past day and night I have more important things on my mind.

Looking him in the eye, I nod. "Ready."

Chapter Eleven

✿❦✿

The next five hours go by in a blur of Aqua Net, pearls, and endless soups, greens, cornbread, biscuits, pineapple upside down cake, and Coca Cola.

My cheeks hurt from smiling, my neck from nodding, and I skirt questions about taking over The Wedding Chapel. The bump on the back of my head throbs, and I feel a migraine coming on.

Mama calls at one point and tells me she's contacted the funeral parlor and Mr. Shackleford will arrange a meeting time the next day. My stomach turns over at the thought.

By three, I'm dead on my feet. Brax makes excuses for me and I say my goodbyes to those still lingering. His mama hasn't made it by yet—her main stove at the restaurant went belly up right before the lunch rush and she's been battling with that since.

A small group of the ladies continue on strong, even after Brax trundles me upstairs to my bedroom. I plop on the bed and he pulls off my shoes—a pair of heels he discovered in Willa's closet and forced me to wear. My aunt and I have the same shoe size, but my feet are killing me all the same.

My hair has resumed its normal messiness, defying Brax's ministrations. My makeup is long past its prime as well after receiving dozens of hugs and air kisses from auxiliary members who still remember me as a little girl.

I don't have the energy to peel off my clothes or wash my face. I fall sideways onto the pillow, Brax's voice already growing distant as my eyes fall like heavy weights. The delicious feeling of the soft pillow makes me sigh. Maybe if I sleep, the migraine will disappear and the knot on the back of my head will shrink.

"I'll check on you later, honey." He draws an afghan over me. "But if you need me at any point, you call me, you hear? Your phone's all charged."

"Mm hmm," I mutter, not even able to get a thank you out.

Arthur and Lancelot jump on the bed, nestling beside me, and I sink into oblivion.

When I wake sometime later the room is dark.

A small, warm body is curled against my back. I hear quiet humming and I smile to myself.

Aunt Willa.

The thought, and the humming, rap on my sleepy brain, bringing me into full consciousness. My heart skitters and I'm frozen. The only light comes from the window with a seat that overlooks the gardens. A partial moon sends soft illumination to kiss the lace curtains and make patterns on the floor.

"Aunt Willa?" I call softly into the shadows of the hallway.

Like a dream, the humming fades. My eyes adjust and I spot a glass of water and my phone on the nightstand. There's also a sticky note.

I reach for it, but can't quite make out the message. Kicking off the afghan wrapped around my legs, I sit up and sling my feet over the edge of the bed. A touch of vertigo hits, but the migraine has gone.

Over my shoulder, I see Lancelot and Arthur cuddled around Tabby.

Tabby! *Hallelujah.*

I sigh with relief that she's back and safe. The previous encounter with her flashes through my mind. I rub the back of my head, the lump no smaller and still sore. Did I imagine her talking to me?

I hold up the sticky note and turn it toward the window, seeing Brax's handwriting. His fine print has long strokes and informs me he found Tabby at the back door. *Must have got hungry*, the message reads.

The alarm clock numbers read a few minutes past eleven. I check my phone and see a voicemail from Mama and a couple of text messages from my friend Winter Whitethorn. She's in Oregon and several hours behind the East Coast.

Mama's message tells me that our appointment with Mordecai Shackleford at Resting Hollow Funeral Parlor is at 10 a.m. the next morning. She asks if I'm coming over for dinner tonight, which I've obviously missed at this hour. Even though I was sleeping, I feel the familiar guilt oozing through my veins. I do need to talk to her, question her again about what she heard at the creek. At this hour, I'm hoping that she's in bed. My questions will have to wait till morning.

I relieve my bladder, wash my face and brush out my hair. I slip into clean pajamas—Brax washed and left the folded pair on the bathroom vanity—and return to the bedroom. Arthur and Lancelot have vanished, and Tabitha is sitting on the antique trunk.

She lifts a paw, licks it, washes her face. All while throwing me a bored look.

My gaze drops to the trunk. "I don't suppose you're going to tell me what's in there?" I turn on the bedside lamp. "Or explain who 'he' is—the man you mentioned at the old homestead—or why he killed my aunt?"

Her yellow eyes, gold in the light, barely glance at me as she continues her face cleaning. A part of me is relieved she doesn't speak. I can chalk up the earlier incident to my concussion.

The other part, the more practical one, is disappointed. If the cat can talk, she might be able to clear up a lot of my questions.

One of the most important blurts right out. "Were you there with her when she died?"

Another flick of the yellow eyes and back to her paw, but her tongue hesitates for a moment as though she understands me. I brace myself, assuming she's going to actually speak.

She doesn't, using her paw to work over one of her ears.

"Come on, Tabitha. If you can talk, now is the time."

She ignores me, moving to lick her forepaw. Frustrated, I let out a heavy sigh and look up toward the heavens. "I don't understand any of this," I tell whoever may be listening. "Aunt Willa, if you're around and can come through, I could use some help."

Tabitha stops washing herself and looks at me as though I'm daft. Maybe I am. No ghost nor naked women appear, no objects in the room decide to speak.

My stomach growls and I rub a hand over my eyes. "Okay then. There's only one thing to do at this late hour."

I head downstairs, flipping on lights as I make my way to the kitchen.

Tabitha follows, meowing, the sound slightly chastising.

As the water in the kettle heats, I inventory the numerous desserts covering the countertop and kitchen table. No surprise there is a plethora of chocolate—my favorite— including cookies, cakes, and candy. Snatching bites here and there, I return to a huge plate of chocolate chip cookies and snag two.

My stomach was too upset earlier to eat, and now in the

quiet of the house I'm content to stuff my face with comfort food as I wander the front rooms.

Arthur and Lancelot jump into their respective spots in the large display windows, tiptoeing around the wedding scenes depicted in them. Across the bride and her woodland setting, two dark shadows, backlit by the streetlight and moon, mimic the cat gargoyles on the porch bannister.

Sentries on watch, all of them. I think about going out to confront the gargoyles and the door knocker but decide it's not worth the chilly night air.

Rosie's desk is piled high with file folders and three-ring binders. Colored sticky notes cover her computer screen and blotter. Pictures of her three dogs are nearly hidden behind all of the work.

My aunt's desk is still pristine and resembles a shrine in the glow of the overhead ceiling light. An eclectic mix of folding chairs have been left on both sides, the energy of the ladies lingering along with their perfumes.

The kettle whistles, and I turn off the front room lights, returning to the kitchen. There, I make a cup of mint tea, start to grab another cookie, and end up taking the whole plate upstairs with me. As Tabitha and I climb the steps, she jets past me, returning to the bedroom.

The trunk is heavier than I expect, and I tug and grunt, sliding it over to the window seat. The pillows and blanket were handmade by my aunt and are the same ones I sunk into as a girl. I make myself comfortable, finishing my cookie as I stare at the trunk.

I spent countless hours in this window seat growing up, lost in grand adventures in the books I read. My favorite series was Nancy Drew, and the collection still sits on the child's desk across the room from me. Every one of her books was read and re-read countless times, leading me to stare out at the gardens and dream about my future life and all the things I wanted to do. Like Nancy, I was going to help people, solve mysteries, triumph over injustice, and put the bad guys away. As I got older, I became fascinated with weddings, drawing intriguing gowns, and imagining dressing brides all over the world who were just as dynamic and adventurous as I was. Ballgowns, mermaid gowns, sleek modern sheaths...I wanted to create cutting-edge designs for brave, spunky heroines.

Tabitha hops up on the seat next to me, eyeing the cookies on the plate. I pin her with my gaze. "Tell me what I need to know," I say to her, "and you can have all the cookies you want."

She cuts her golden eyes to me then lies down next to my leg, staring at the trunk.

Well, it was worth a try.

The way she stares, infatuated at the trunk, reminds me of the look on Logan's face when he saw Prissy this morning and thought we might put on a show.

"Alright." I take one last sip of tea to fortify myself before I flip the metal latch in the center of the trunk. My breath catches in my chest and I force myself to take a deep breath and ignore my fluttering pules. "Let's see what secrets are inside this thing."

The dome lid squeaks as I lift it, like nails on a chalkboard. I flinch, and Tabby's nails extend, clawing into the padded seat under us. The top of the trunk is filled with a few old books, some of my aunt's costume jewelry, a few random trinkets.

False bottom, I remember. I shift things around, searching for a way to find it.

Sure enough, with another squeak, this one deeper, I find a lip under the memorabilia and give a tug.

As moonlight and lamplight converge and dance together to illuminate the contents below, I stare somewhat dumbfounded at the collection of items inside.

And then as realization dawns, an icy shiver races up my spine.

Chapter Twelve

✦❀✦

"What in heaven's name?" My eyes skim over the contents several times, cataloguing each one.

A glass ball catches the moonlight, a feather boa waves at me as if there's a breeze. Several books, some seemingly older than others, scarves, candles, a deck of tarot cards.

My fingers rifle through the scarves, one of them covered with gold coins. It tinkles. I lift it out and examine the see-through material, the sound of the coins invoking images of belly dancers. I lift out a wig of long, dark hair, a peasant skirt, a bright orange shawl.

Sitting back, I let go a relieved laugh. This is nothing more than a kid's dress-up trunk. Not one I ever got to play with, but certainly nothing to cause the anxiety I'd felt about opening it.

The icy sensation on my skin doesn't go away, though. The tinkling scarf meant to go around a dancer's hips suddenly feels heavier in my hands.

Tabitha stretches a paw out and bats at a black leather-bound book. It's long and thin, with a leather cord wrapped around it, keeping it shut.

"Ledger" is stamped in gold on the front cover.

Setting the scarf aside, I reach for the book. Tabitha sits up straight and looks me directly in the eyes, as if encouraging me. Arthur and Lancelot mosey in and jump up onto the bed, watching with something akin to anticipation. It's almost as if Tabby has called them.

I remove the band and open the book. Columns fill the pages, entries on each line. Across the top, the headings list Day, Name, Service, Fee, and whether payment was received or in arrears. The dates span back years; the names seem to be made up, and all sound like food—Maple Taffy, White Eggs, Candy Lane.

A child's game, I think, ready to toss the book back into the trunk. Aunt Willa and I used to make up codes for people when we wanted to talk about them without them knowing it. It was simple, innocent fun.

That's all this is, I tell myself. Before I close the book, my eye catches on one of the services listed: house clearing. I continue to go down the column.

Hex breaking.

Great grandmother's ring—found.

Baby prediction: boy.

Protection prayer and charm.

And one that chills my bones—*Evicted evil spirit.*

I slam the book shut. This is definitely not a child's game.

I drop the book on the seat and look at Tabby. "What is this nonsense?"

She blinks at me, blank.

I'm talking to a cat. Worse, I expect her to answer.

I've lost it. My marbles are gone.

From inside the trunk, another thick-bound volume awaits, the binding old and worn. There are metal grommets in the corners and a lock on the book, giving it a somewhat gothic appearance.

Shaking off the fear the other book has left in my mind, I hesitate to take it out but can't resist the draw. The thick book's lock is fashioned like a cat head—one that matches the door knocker out front.

The keyhole is the cat's mouth, and my memory flashes. The necklace! Aunt Willa's key pendant was shaped like a cat's curling tale.

I never knew what the key went to. She always told me it was just a necklace. Dollars to doughnuts, it went to this book.

The tome weighs a ton and covers my lap with its generous size. I try to open it, but the lock doesn't give.

I pry a finger under one worn corner, attempting to read the yellowed page underneath. I can't make out much, but I see faded script. Tabby leans over and licks my hand, startling me and making me jump. An orange pamphlet falls from between the pages.

A cartoonish toad with a crown is emblazoned on the top. *Thorny Toad Psychedelic Saturdays* is stamped underneath it. There's a list of names and a date from several years before. I scan the list, realizing these are attractions for this Saturday night get-together. My focus is drawn to Mina the Medium.

Mina, as in *Wilhelmina*?

Aunt Willa went by Willa and Willa Rae. I never heard anyone call her Mina. I replace the book in the trunk, chewing my bottom lip and wondering if I could pry the lock open with a knife, or a letter opener. Maybe a screwdriver? I set the orange flyer on top of the books and wonder what Aunt Willa was playing at.

Suddenly, Tabby meows and I see her looking out the window. She arches her back, hair standing up all along her spine.

"What is it, girl?" I brush back the lace curtain.

Moonlight winks off metal on the other side of the hedgerow fence in Mr. Upton's yard. Dirt flies through the air.

I scrunch my forehead, narrowing my eyes and leaning as far over as the window will allow. The tip of a shovel flings dirt, once, twice, three times, behind the tall barrier of boxwoods lining the fence between our properties. If I remember correctly, that area's his prized gardenia garden.

"Why is he planting something in the middle of the night?" I wonder out loud.

I know he's had trouble in the past with moles. Aunt Willa did, too, so maybe he's on the path of one of those pesky critters. They seemed to like this area close to the creek.

Like my aunt, Mr. Upton has added rich garden soil to his yard over the years and his gardenias have thrived. He's won awards at the county fair and some of Willa's brides have used that corner of his garden for more pictures. There was always a slight competition between him and my aunt for who could have the most beautiful garden.

I'm considering wandering over to ask him if he saw or heard anything unusual last night when the doorbell rings, making me jump.

Chapter Thirteen

❧

L ogan Cross is on the front porch.

"What's up?" I ask, after cracking open the door.

He gives me a crooked grin. "Saw the lights on. Couldn't sleep? You okay?"

"Define okay." I think about talking cats, the ledger and the flyer. Mina the Medium.

The grin broadens and he throws a casual hand up on the frame. "Rough day with the ladies auxiliary, I take it?"

"Good guess."

"They mean well."

He looks like a lawyer tonight in a dress shirt, tie, and slacks. "No one should look that good at this time of night." I give him another once-over. "Aren't you off the clock by now?"

"Long day," he says on an exasperated sigh. He loosens his tie. "The Pumpkins and Peach Wine Charity Dinner was tonight with my parents."

The wine tour on Sunday stretches over three counties and is a huge tourist draw to the area in conjunction with the festival. The Cross Winery has won dozens of awards for their specialty wine, Peachy Keen Pinot, and they hold a charity dinner every year before the tour, the family being well known for their philanthropy.

"Let him in." The whisper near my ear makes me suck in a breath.

The door knocker's talking again.

Logan doesn't seem to hear it, and I guess that's a good thing, although it might confirm I'm simply crazy. Easing the door open another inch, I silently bemoan the fact Logan is once more seeing me in my pajamas with no makeup and frizzy hair.

But a plan to get a few answers hits, and we are now alone. "Could I interest you in some ham and beans? Cookies?"

"Real food? Yes, please." He follows me into the house. "That catered stuff Mom has at these things looks appetizing, but it never fills me up. Got any cornbread to go with the ham and beans?"

In the kitchen, I glance around at the countertop selections. "I saw some earlier." I point to a blue glass dish with a plastic lid. A piece of masking tape on it reads "Teresa Maples."

"Excellent." Logan rubs his hands together. "Terry makes the best cornbread."

A split-second passes, my focus zeroing in on her name. There's something about it…

"Hey, you okay?" Logan asks.

"Yes." My voice is a little too bright as I try to cover my mind travel. "Just trying to place her face."

He goes on to describe her, who she's related to, stuff about her brother—an all-star basketball player at Thornhollow High —and other stuff I don't really listen to. I stick two bowls of ham and bean soup in the microwave.

As they heat, Logan gathers silverware, once more revealing he knows this kitchen well. I grab out plates, my brain still stuck on Teresa's name.

I pour sweet tea for both of us, not bothering to ask Logan

what he wants, but he doesn't complain. I'm struck by the fact that this pitcher of tea is the last my aunt will ever make.

Logan sheds the tie and unbuttons the top of his shirt, then rolls up the sleeves to his elbows, revealing strong forearms that are beautifully tan. The cats meander in and check their bowls.

"You found Tabby," he says, smiling.

"Brax did. Said she showed up at the back door at dinnertime."

We dig into the food, neither of us talking for several quiet moments. I nearly moan at how good it all tastes.

Coming up for air, I wipe my mouth and ask Logan how much the charity raised. He tells me about one of the wine vintages that sold in the silent auction for nearly $800 tonight.

"That's crazy." I've never understood people's fascination with expensive wine. A five-dollar bottle tastes about the same to me as the pricey stuff.

He seems to agree, nodding his head. "Good for the kids though."

The Cross charity grants money every year to our local kids' club. The charity supplies sports uniforms, band instruments, and funds educational trips for many of the children in the area.

Around us at the table are multiple dishes of dessert items. Logan fishes through several, snagging a homemade turtle candy and chomping down on the yummy mix of pecans, caramel, and chocolate.

"Are you having trouble sleeping?" he asks again, pointing to my pajamas.

"Nah. I napped, but I have a lot on my mind. Questions with no answers."

He inhales another candy. "You want to know why, right? Why Willa Rae? She was such a pillar of the community and seems young to have died so soon. It doesn't seem fair, does it?"

No, it doesn't. "Actually,"—I push away my plate and pin him with a stare—"What I want to know right now is why you have a key to this house?"

Chapter Fourteen

L ogan's gaze is steady and calm. "She needed money and asked me to buy the house from her."

My stomach drops. "She sold you The Wedding Chapel? Her *home*?"

He puts up a hand in a *wait* gesture. "Not the business or the grounds. Just the house. She planned to buy it back, and I've been putting her rent checks toward it."

"What did she need money for?" And why didn't she come to me? "Is the business in trouble?"

"She wouldn't say." He shrugs. "I suggested she take out a short-term loan, but she refused. Said she didn't want anyone but me, her lawyer, knowing she needed help, especially the busybodies at the bank."

Help with what? My mind reels with possibilities. Was she sick? Bankrupt? Again, I feel distraught she didn't come to me.

"A copy of our agreement should be in her files." He's watching me carefully. "If you don't find it, I'll make another."

I'm stunned speechless. After everything I've experienced in the past twenty-four hours, this might be the most perplexing.

"Welcome to the Twilight Zone," I mutter. Making a pillow of my hands, I rest my forehead on them.

Logan stands, removing our plates and taking them to the sink to rinse them. I hear the squeak of the dishwasher door as he sticks them inside.

Returning, he places a warm, sturdy hand on my shoulder. "I should get going. You need rest."

He digs in a pocket and places a key on the table next to my elbow. "You keep this. It'll make you feel better. And I don't need it with you here."

I lift my head. Nothing will make me feel better, but his gesture actually does ease my tension a bit.

I sit up fully. "Mama heard Willa arguing with someone at the creek before she died, but never saw the person. Do you have any idea who it might have been?"

His hand slides off my shoulder, and he frowns. "No idea. People came and went from here all the time."

I rise and see him to the door. The house seems too quiet, too...empty. I almost hate to let him go.

At the door, he gives me that steady gaze again. "Get some sleep. Let's talk tomorrow. But if you need anything tonight, I'm just across the street."

"Sure."

I watch him go down the path, through the gate, and cross the street to this place. After I make sure he's safely inside, I lock the door.

Then I sit at Aunt Willa's desk and start looking for clues as to why she would sell Logan the family home.

Chapter Fifteen

❧❧❧

By 9 a.m., I'm showered, dressed and feeling more like myself. No ghosts, no talking cats, and I've spoken to my boss to secure time off, had a chat with Winter about the ghost activity—which has reassured me about my psychic abilities—and been through all of Aunt Willa's financial accounts.

Business accounts anyway. I can't find her personal banking information, but between Mama and Rosie, one of them should know where her bank statements are.

Aunt Willa was old school and didn't bank online. There are a few credit card statements in her files, but nothing looks out of place. The charges and payments align with recent wedding expenses.

Rosie arrives ten minutes before Mama. Her little dog is once again in her tote as she settles at her desk. I hand her a cup of coffee. "Do you know why Aunt Willa sold this house to Logan Cross?"

Her face pinches, the cup stopping in mid-air on its way to her pumpkin-colored lips. "She did *what?*"

The little dog, Fern, hides her head in the tote.

"You didn't know?"

She sets down the cup with a *thunk* that nearly splashes coffee over the sides. "Heavens no. Why did she do that?"

"Your guess is better than mine. And I'd appreciate it if you'd keep this between us. Logan said she needed cash, but I haven't figured out why. He claims he doesn't know. I've been through the business accounts and everything looks solid, but I can't find her personal stuff. You wouldn't happen to know where she kept that, would you?"

"I believe Miss Willa has a lockbox at the bank. Maybe she kept it there? Would Miss Della know?"

Seems inconvenient. "I hate to suggest such a thing, but Logan has a key to the house, and…"

I let the accusation hang between us. Rosie catches my drift. "No way. Logan's a good guy. Why would he take Miss Willa's bank statements?"

I feel like a heel even insinuating it. "I don't know, but with everything that's happened I'm a little suspicious of a whole lot of people." I shrug and see her rear back as if offended. "Not you, Rosie. I know you loved Willa like I did."

"You bet your Sunday dinner I did." She shakes her head and champions Logan again. "Logan would never do anything underhanded."

This reassures me a little. I can't stomach thinking he would hurt my aunt or steal papers from her house after her demise. I make a mental note to ask Mama for ideas and cross my fingers she knows where those bank statements might be.

Rosie and I spend the next few minutes discussing the possibilities for the estate, and I try to reassure her that The Wedding Chapel will continue in business for now. "I'm not letting everything Aunt Willa worked so hard for go down the tubes. We're keeping this place open as long as possible."

As the words leave my mouth, I wonder how I'm going to accomplish that, considering my boss only agreed to one week off before I need to return to work. Fall is always busy for our salon with brides planning for Valentine's Day weddings as well as those getting fitted for holiday ones.

"Ava, I honestly can't believe she wouldn't tell me if she needed money," Rosie says.

"You and me both. Was she acting odd lately? Any change in her routine? Did she seem healthy to you?"

Fern climbs out of the tote and Rosie cradles her in her arms. "I worked with that woman five days a week and sometimes on Saturdays when we had a big event. She was like a mother to me."

Rosie's eyes well with tears, and she nuzzles Fern. "I swear I never saw anything different. I know they said she had a lot of anxiety, and she definitely worked too hard, but I thought the meds were helping. She never seemed overly anxious to me, or sick in any way. She was healthier than I am…at least that's what I thought. Do you think she had cancer or something? That she just didn't tell any of us?"

I've heard stories about folks who have terminal illnesses and don't tell their family because they don't want them to worry. It does seem like something Aunt Willa might do. "You or Mama would have noticed if she was sick, I'm sure." I attempt to relieve her worry as I walk to the front display window on her side of the office. The sun is shining on the fallen leaves out front and glinting off the wagon display in the yard. "She sure loved this time of year."

"This and Christmas. And Valentine's." Rosie chuckles. "Actually, she loved all the holidays."

Across the street, I see Logan moving around in his office. "When you left here the day she died, was there anyone else around?"

"I had to leave early and take little Mikey to see Dr. Abernathy. Mikey threw up at school and was running a fever. Doc said it was something he ate, nothing serious, but because of the fever, I needed to watch him overnight."

She joins me at the window, Fern now at her feet. Arthur and Lancelot are curled up near Snow White's red shoes in the window, and they eye the small dog with a mixture of annoyance and boredom. "Mikey has food allergies, which we never would have found out about if it weren't for Willa."

"Is that so?"

Rosie continues with a nod. "My hubby's insurance wouldn't cover the cost of testing, and Willa gave me the money for it. I swear on the Blessed Mother, she saved his life—and my sanity. He's so much healthier now since we keep him away from dairy and corn."

I imagine life without those two things and internally cringe. "Aunt Willa was a generous person."

"I paid her back," Rosie assures me. "Every month, I made an installment. Some of the other folks, they couldn't afford to pay back the money she gave them."

I swivel to face her as Mama's sedan pulls to the curb outside. "Other folks?"

Rosie picks up Fern. "Miss Willa was always helping people out. There's this homeless couple with dogs who come through town every month. They wanted to get married back in the summer but had no money, so she had them get their license at the courthouse then brought them back here and married them herself. No charge. We used our props and even the dogs got to be in the ceremony."

My aunt was a wedding officiant, and she'd performed quite a few weddings over the years. Baptisms, too, and even a funeral here and there.

Tabitha appears at my feet. She makes a disgusted noise in her throat as if she's hacking up a hairball. She hisses at the Chihuahua before she jumps up with Arthur and Lancelot.

Lancelot begins to clean her fur, and she stretches like a queen enjoying a massage.

Rosie squeezes Fern a little tighter. "Your aunt was always doing things like that. She didn't talk about who she lent money to, but everybody in town knew she did."

"Did she have any enemies?" Mama is making her way up the stone path. She's squeezed her generous proportions into a bright blue two-piece suit, the skirt hitting modestly below her knees. She's on her cell, her empty hand waving in the air as she speaks and marches up the porch steps.

"Enemies?" Rosie echoes. "Not that I know of. Why?"

I tell her about the person who may have been arguing with Aunt Willa at the creek. Her eyes grow wide. Fern struggles against her chest, her tiny feet pawing at Rosie's face to get her attention.

Rosie kisses her nose and strokes the dog's tiny face. "Well…"

Mama stops on the porch, still talking on her cell phone, and looks out over the yard. I can hear exasperation in her voice, and the hand waves through the air once more as if emphasizing something.

When Rosie doesn't finish her sentence, I face her. "Well, what?"

"The police asked me about it." Rosie's gaze goes to Mama on the porch, then back to me. "I don't like to speak ill of anyone, but you know about Priscilla, right?"

I swing the door open for my mother and she jets in, patting me on the face. Still conversing with whoever's on the other end of the call, she hustles over to Aunt Willa's desk and plops down. "No, I told you that will not work… Yes, 2 p.m. Not a minute earlier."

After closing the door, I return to Rosie's side. "I know about Priscilla's competitive streak. Was she here that day?"

She shakes her head, her brows drawn in deep thought. "No, but that's the only enemy I can think of."

"Logan didn't come by that day, did he?"

Her nose scrunches, as if annoyed I'm back on that train. "Yes, but..."

"But what?" She looks away. "Rosie, tell me."

Her gaze comes back to mine. "He did come by, and your aunt went out back with him to discuss something. Guess it was private. He left shortly afterward, seeming a little upset."

My breath catches inside my sternum. "He didn't mention that."

"Logan would never hurt anyone, especially not Willa."

"Of course not." My voice comes out strained and quiet. My throat is tight. "Can you think of anyone else I should speak to who might know what was going on with my aunt?"

"There's Doc."

I hesitate for a second, remembering how fond he seemed of my aunt when we discussed her. "Dr. Abernathy? He didn't like Aunt Willa?"

Rosie chuckles, her dog laying her head on Rosie's collarbone. "Just the opposite, actually. Doc was in love with her."

Chapter Sixteen

❦

"What did I miss?" Mama hurries to our side of the front room, now done with her call.

I'm still a bit flabbergasted. "Dr. Abernathy was in love with Aunt Willa? I mean, I guessed he liked her after our talk at the clinic, but love?"

Thunder booms outside, the weather deciding to get in on the conversation. The cats scatter, Fern hides, and Mama rolls her eyes. "I need coffee."

I instinctively point toward the kitchen. "I reheated Donna Sherman's peach cobbler and some biscuits, too, if you want them."

As she scuttles away, punching buttons on her phone once more, Rosie tells me, "They've been dating all year."

Another thing she didn't tell me. I feel a sting of hurt—a lot of hurt, to be honest. Apparently, my aunt was full of secrets.

"He was nuts about her." Rosie walks in her three-inch heels back to her desk, tucking the dog onto her lap as she resumes her seat. "He was always bringing her gifts, chastising her for working so hard, trying to get her to marry him."

I nearly choke. "Marry him!"

My uncle Saddler died when I was only six. I barely remember him, but Aunt Willa talked about him all the time. She has pictures of him on the bookshelves and in her room on the nightstand. Through her stories I've always felt his presence, and I never imagined her falling for anyone else.

He was a carpenter and built the bookshelves in all the rooms, the rocking chairs on the front porch. He made me a cedar chest that's at my place in Atlanta. "And how did she feel about Doc?"

Rosie sorts through a stack of files on her desk and checks her calendar. "I think she liked him a whole lot. She definitely enjoyed his company. Beyond that?" She shrugs. "I used to love hearing them laugh on the back porch when he'd stop by unexpectedly to see her and she'd sneak him out there."

I stand slightly frozen, trying to come to terms with this new information. Another roll of thunder outside is followed by the crack of lightning.

My mind whizzes with possibilities. "Was he here yesterday?"

"Nope. Why?"

I walk toward her desk. "Did they ever argue?"

Rosie gives me a look that would melt iron.

"Sorry. It's just…a lot to take in."

"Doc would never hurt anyone, especially your aunt."

I hope she's right.

"Ava," Mama summons from the kitchen. "Where's my creamer?"

"Coming." To Rosie I say, "If you think of anyone else…"

She nods, locating the folder she was looking for and booting up her computer, "You'll be the first to know."

In the kitchen, Mama sorts through the fridge. "There's so much food in here I can't find a blessed thing."

I reach across her to the door's top shelf and retrieve what she's looking for.

"Oh, there it is." She whisks it from me and loads her mug with the liquid. Plunking down at the table, she places a napkin in her lap. Her face is a little tired but anticipatory as she eyes the bowl of cobbler in front of her. "How did you know I need breakfast?"

Because I've been taking care of you ever since Dad left, I think but don't say out loud. She's mostly been on her own for the past few years, so in good conscience I can't hold a grudge. I just give her a weak smile. "I've always known what you needed."

My mother is the undisputed queen of eye rolls. I don't need to see the award-winning one she shoots my way as I refill my coffee—I feel it. "Always so dramatic, Ava."

"Wonder who I learned it from?" I take the seat across from her, watching her dive into the food. She issues a sigh as the first spoonful hits her taste buds.

"I want to do an autopsy," I tell her.

Her chewing stops and she looks at me as if I've morphed into an alien right in front of her eyes. "Whatever in heaven's name for?"

"You heard her arguing with someone before she died. Yesterday, I found her necklace in the creek, broken, and the key pendant missing. Mama, I think it's possible she didn't die from a heart attack."

Mama waves both hands in the air between us as if throwing up a magical wall. "I was mistaken—just..." She shivers visibly. "It was such a shock, Ava. Totally upended everything. I imagined it, that argument. That's all."

She forces a half-hearted smile. It doesn't reach her eyes, no matter how hard she tries.

"That's not true." I reach across the table and pat her arm. "We need answers and peace of mind. If there was foul play surrounding Aunt Willa's death, an autopsy will reveal it."

"No, I won't have it."

I expected as much. "Did Aunt Willa have any enemies here in town?"

Mama sucks in a sharp breath and pulls away from my hand, glancing at her cobbler with a twinge of longing.

This is my relationship with my mother in a nutshell. I make her face uncomfortable truths and have a knack of ruining the few pleasurable moments she allows herself.

"We all have enemies," she says under her breath, her palms now resting on the table. Her lips form a thin line as she stares at the food. "There was no foul play. She had a weak heart and she died, Ava. It was just bad luck."

Was it? The words burn in my throat.

Her gaze lifts to me, as if she heard my thought. "The police looked into it and found nothing. I spoke to Detective Jones this morning. I was the only witness to hear anything, and you know what your father always said about witnesses…"

My father, the former cop, pontificated a great deal about the law. I bet he and Logan would have had some interesting conversations if Daddy were still in town. "Witness testimony can be helpful but is often unreliable."

A nod. "That's what Detective Jones reiterated to me, and I'm sure he's right." Another forced smile. "I was under a lot of stress that day and whatever I heard, I was wrong about it."

Mama's always under stress; life as mayor of a small town made her successful but also slightly crazy. The anxiety should be enough to trigger her own heart attack. "Are you taking your blood pressure meds?"

Her eyes flit away and back. "Of course. I'm fit as a fiddle. And I believed Willa was, too, but, as I said, she had a weak heart."

There is a double meaning behind my mother's tone—not only Willa's physical heart was weak, but Mama saw her generosity as a weakness as well.

I fortify myself with a big sip of coffee and play with the cup.

"I'm ordering an autopsy. I'm sorry that upsets you, but I have to."

She rears back and dramatically places a hand on her head. "Lord, give me patience." She casts her eyes heavenward before glaring at me. "To what end, Ava?"

I tug the letter from under the cobbler pie dish on the table. I tucked it there earlier, preparing to share it with her once she'd had coffee and sugar. "Something *was* going on. She sold this house to Logan Cross, and she sent me this note right before she died."

A *pfft* noise vibrates her lips. "She would never sell this house. It's been in our family since the founding of the town."

"Apparently she did."

She shakes her head, dismissing my argument, and opens the letter. Her eyes skim it, her face tightening with every line.

"There's foul play surrounding her death," I insist, "and I'm not going to rest until I figure it out." I down more coffee, giving me strength. "If you have an explanation for any of this, I'm listening. If not, I'm ordering that autopsy today."

As if the paper has caught fire, she drops it on top of her bowl and scoots her chair back. "Come on. We're gonna be late to meet Mr. Shackleford."

"Why did she need money, Mama?"

She shoots to her feet. "Who told you she did?"

"Mama, she sold the house to Logan in order to raise funds. Yes, I asked if he knew why, and he claims she wouldn't tell him."

"Ridiculous." She starts to flee the kitchen she's so upset, but then stops in the doorway. "If she needed money, she would have come to me. She probably just wanted to have more to give away, silly sister of mine."

The dismissive attitude raises my hackles. "She was a generous person, but I can't see her getting herself into so much debt she'd have to sell this house."

"I have no idea what she was thinking. She didn't exactly confide in me." She takes a step back into the room and lowers her voice. "All I know is that the voices in her head were getting louder and more persistent." Snark fills her next words. "Maybe one of *them* told her to sell the house. Maybe that's who she was arguing with at the creek. An invisible ghost!"

I hear the phone on Rosie's desk ring and she picks it up, repeating the business slogan, "'The Wedding Chapel, from flowers and food to the happy I dos.' How may I help you?"

The snarl on my mother's face is to hide her fear. I try to ease it as best I can while still honoring my aunt. "Aunt Willa had a gift, Mama. I have it, too. Are we both nuts? Possibly, but you and I owe it to her to prove one way or the other if she died of natural causes."

With another intake of breath and an angry huff, Mama resumes her march to the front door. "I'll meet you at the funeral parlor."

"I assure you everything's right on schedule," Rosie says into the phone. "Ava and I are handling it. I'll check on it now and call you as soon as I can, Miranda. Yes, I promise."

Trailing after Mama, I try to stop her. "Just let me grab my purse and we can ride together."

Always an enigma with her emotions, Mama turns and throws her arms around me. "I know you want to do right by your aunt, but there's no mystery to any of this, Ava. Just drop it. You're not responsible for our family or the town. Or any of that other baloney she's filled your head with. After the funeral, you can go back to your life in Atlanta and enjoy it."

She releases me so abruptly I nearly lose my balance, and then she's out the door.

Swiveling to retrieve my coat and purse, I set my jaw. Rosie's done with her call. "Who do I contact about ordering an autopsy?" I ask her.

"Got the number for the county coroner right here." She holds up a sticky note.

This is one of the many reasons Aunt Willa adored her—she's efficient and loyal.

I take the yellow piece of paper and shrug on my trench coat, shoving the number in a pocket. "Thanks. Do we have appointments today?"

Rosie's eyes light up with the realization that I'm helping, at least for now. "Penny Calhoun at three for a consult. Otherwise everything is pretty clear."

"I'll be here."

"I have to run to the country club to check on the ballroom for the Burnett/Durham wedding. Miranda said they're having electrical issues or something, which could be a big problem for the reception."

I open the front door, feeling the cool air and smelling damp leaves. "Good. Keep me posted."

She nods, rising and sticking Fern in the tote. "Also, you have parade practice at four-thirty. The chamber respectfully requests you take Willa's place to lead it."

I bite the inside of my bottom lip. "Can't someone else do it?"

Rosie winks at me. "I think Willa would want you to. Plus, if there *is* a killer roaming around here, he'll most likely be there."

She's right. "You're brilliant."

A modest shrug lifts her shoulders. "Hey, I read Nancy Drew, too."

We share a smile and I hightail it to the funeral parlor.

Chapter Seventeen

❦

The smell of ripe fruit and embalming fluid hits my nose as I enter Resting Hollow. For some reason, Mr. Shackleford and his wife must think the scent of mango and pineapple covers the odor of death.

Outside the harsh thunderstorm has trailed away, leaving only a light rain and humidity behind. A soft, subtle *bing-bong* chimes overhead, announcing my presence as I push through the double glass doors. They are heavy and slow, making a swishing noise as I enter.

The hallway is wide with neat rows of hangers on each wall, lined up like soldiers ready for the coats of mourners. Light gospel music filters through unseen speakers overhead, and I pass a vignette with a small table and two chairs in an alcove that leads down another corridor to the bathrooms.

As I cruise past a viewing room on the quiet, plush carpeting, I see a man on a stepladder hanging a large painting on the paneled wall. His head is shaved on both sides with a thick carpet of bleached hair running from his forehead to neck. With his tawny skin and assorted tattoos on his neck, I have the brief impression of a skunk.

His head swivels, dark eyes meeting mine. Muscled arms bulge from the weight of the framed painting.

My brain supplies his name—Timmy Shackleford. Younger than me by several years, I try to recall what I know about him. "Good morning."

A flash of something crosses his face, almost like surprise. "Morning. Sorry about Miss Willa."

Football player, my brain supplies. He went somewhere not too far away. Alabama? He was scholarship material, if I recall, but hurt himself and ended up back home, his dreams of going pro dashed.

"Thank you." He's still holding up the painting. "Do you need help with that?"

The former football star doesn't seem fazed by my offer, even though his muscled arms are twice the size of mine. He slowly shakes his head. "They're waiting for you."

On cue, I hear Mama's voice, "Ava? We're back here."

Steeling my resolve, I nod to Timmy and move on. I wonder if he's happy here. Does he find it peaceful in this place or depressing?

A backward glance makes me stop in my tracks. Timmy is going through the same motions as when I walked in—hanging the painting—but as I watch, the gilt-framed picture returns to its place propped against the wall, him at the bottom of the ladder. He climbs the rungs, bends down and heaves it up. Prepares to hang it. In a blink, the scene repeats. This time, from the bottom of the ladder, he glances at me, sensing I'm still there. A sadness fills his eyes before he gives a slight shrug and once more repeats the actions.

Timmy is a...ghost.

"Ava!" Another clear summons.

"Coming," I call, wondering how in the heck to help Mordecai's dead son who's caught in some kind of spiritual loop. How did I not know he was dead?

The meeting room is adjacent to the kitchen. The smell of coffee teases my nose, thankfully blocking out the other scents. I find Mama and Mr. Shackleford waiting at a folding table. A box of tissues and a vase of plastic flowers decorates the center.

"There you are." Mama pats a folding chair next to her. "We need to get a move on here."

I remove my coat. "I'm sorry about Timmy," I tell Mr. Shackleford. "I didn't realize he'd passed."

As I drop my coat over the back of a chair, the gray-haired man looks slightly caught off guard. "Why, thank you. It was an unfortunate accident." A shake of his head and his features sour. "Awful painkillers—never could get him off of them."

The folding chair is cold and hard as I sit. I'm sad for him and wondering why Timmy is hanging around. "Did he work here with you?"

Mr. Shackleford's eyes glaze. Under the table, Mama pinches my leg. "He was my only son—I had such high hopes for him. I wanted him to take over the business."

Mama slides her coffee cup toward me, then an open book showing various types of caskets. "I think Willa Rae would have wanted this oak casket with a copper vault."

Mr. Shackleford pulls himself together. "The copper package is our top of the line."

In my ear, I hear a voice. "I want a white casket. Hot pink satin interior."

I glance around and frown.

Shackleford and Mama both follow my gaze. "What's wrong?" Mama says.

"Nothing...I thought I heard..." I shake my head. "Aunt Willa wants a white casket, I think, and a hot pink satin liner."

Mama lifts an accusatory brow. "Stop that," she threatens under her breath.

I flip through a couple of pages, seeing a beautiful white one that should fit the bill.

"Yes!" My aunt's voice is clear in my ear. "Isn't that a stunner?"

I tap the photo. "This one. She wants this one."

"And forget the copper," she demands. "Go with the cheap concrete vault. But I want pink to lie on."

In the silence, I repeat what I've heard. Mama's chest swells and she smooths her countenance. "You would make Jesus cuss some days, Ava. Please stop playing around. You made your point—you and I will discuss this *stuff*"—she says the word like I'm forcing her to swallow bitter cough syrup —"after we're done here. Right now, we need to make these arrangements."

She nods at Mr. Shackleford to continue. His discerning eyes linger on me for a moment. "Ah, the white casket is a popular one—it has inlaid roses carved on the top."

Mama looks like she's going to explode. Her lips work as she attempts a polite response.

"Perfect." I hear more of Aunt Willa's instructions, though I don't see her, and they seem to tumble out of my mouth. "For the casket flowers, she wants a spray of red roses and white gardenias with sprigs of fall leaves tucked in with them. Betty Lee has some—she'll know what I—I mean, *Aunt Willa* wants."

Both of them stare at me slack-jawed.

Winter is always telling me I need to embrace my gift. It's always strongest here in this town among these people. Even though I avoid coming home for this very reason, I'm tired of fighting it. "I need to talk to you," I tell my aunt.

"You *are* talking to us." Mama's face contorts with worry. She thinks I'm losing it for real. She gives Mr. Shackleford an apologetic smile. "It's that hit she took to her head yesterday. Doc says she has a concussion."

"I'll contact Betty Lee and place the order for you," Mr. Shackleford says to me. "We can set up the visitation for Saturday evening. Since Wilhelmina was such a pillar of the community, we should consider a second visitation on Sunday afternoon."

At lease he doesn't think I'm crazy. Or maybe he does but he's too polite to act like it. I give him a thankful look. "Sorry, but that won't work for me. I have the Burnett/Durham wedding on Saturday and the wine tour on Sunday."

Outside in the hall, I swear I see something move. It passes and I continue, sending my gaze around for Aunt Willa, just in case she makes an appearance. "Plus, the autopsy won't be done until Monday."

Mama gasps. On the way over, I called the number Rosie gave me for the county office and they promptly emailed the form I needed to fill out. In the parking lot, before I came in, I emailed it back.

My mother's eyes close and she sighs warily. Shackleford frowns, checks his notes, and looks up at her. "I'm sorry, I didn't know there was going to be an autopsy."

Aunt Willa's voice swoops past me again, startling me. "Put me in the watercolor dress—and I want 'Amazing Grace' sung. Your mama knows which dress I'm talking about. And tell her not to waste money on a bunch of other flowers. It's not like I can enjoy them."

It's so good to hear her voice, even if she *is* a ghost. I smile as I relay the instructions. A heavy, pregnant silence again fills the charged air between us.

Mr. Shackleford shifts uncomfortably, his eyes darting between me and Mama. He's worried she's going to start yelling at me, but I know her better than that. She does not lose her cool, no matter what, even if she does get aggravated.

Sure enough, she scrutinizes my face then scans the room as if double-checking to see if Aunt Willa is actually here. I see the shadow move in the hall again, a female figure floating past the open doorway. Mama doesn't seem to notice, and for some reason I'm relieved.

Mabel Shackleford, Mordecai's wife, bops her head in. "Excuse me for interrupting." She nods at me and Mama. "Barbara Fay Reedsy finally passed, God bless her, and her family's on the way to set up arrangements. It's been such a hard couple of weeks on them. I just couldn't put them off. They'll be here soon, and I figured you were nearly done."

Ah-ha. The ghost floating around the hall might just be Barbara.

Mama, morphing into mayor now, makes a sad face. "I knew she was doing poorly. We're wrapping things up right now."

Mabel disappears and her husband begins gathering his papers. "I believe I have what I need for now. I'll work out the details for the service for next week with Reverend Stout, and once the autopsy is complete we'll firm up the visitation times."

He rises, as do I, and he shakes my hand. "Good to see you, Ava, although I'm sorry about the circumstances." He puts a hand on Mama's shoulder. "Mayor."

When he's gone, Mama continues to sit, staring at nothing, although her gaze is on the table. "Is she still here?" she asks so quietly I almost don't catch it.

"Aunt Willa?" I call discreetly. I hope that Mama's coming around and I can quit carrying this burden alone. I'm so grateful for Winter, since she's the only one I can talk to about this stuff.

Mama worries the ring on her left hand. "If it's really her, ask her to relate something that only I would know."

Mama is a skeptic, obviously, but I can't say I blame her. "I'm not sure where she went." I reach for my coat, my aunt's sudden absence annoying me. This is our chance! Together, we can convince Mama that having the gift of mediumship is not a curse. "But she *was* here, Mama. I didn't make any of that up."

Aunt Willa's voice seems to fly by me again. "My sister wants proof, does she? Fine. Tell her I know the real reason she kicked your daddy out and made him leave town."

My stomach lurches. "Daddy?"

Mama's head rises with a sharp snap. She claimed my father left to follow his dream of becoming a rock star. A stupid, useless dream, according to her, that she chalked up to an early mid-life crisis.

With a thick tongue and a chest filled with dread, I relay Aunt Willa's message. Mama's eyes widen with fear.

"Got her attention, now don't we?" Aunt Willa chuckles.

I know I shouldn't waste this opportunity to confirm whether or not her death was accidental, but all I can think of at the moment is my father. The last time I saw Daddy was at the end of summer when he crashed at my place for a night after a gig in Atlanta. His hair is prematurely gray, but he could easily pass for someone my age. "What about Dad?" I ask hesitantly. "Tell me the truth about why you made him leave."

Mama looks tongue-tied; her mouth opens to speak and then closes again without saying a word. Her lips tighten, and then she looks up toward the ceiling. "Willa, don't," she demands quite clearly.

"It's time you know," my aunt says to me.

I grind my teeth. "Know what?"

"Ask your mother about the curse." Aunt Willa's voice begins to fade. "Sorry, I don't have the energy to stick around. Ask her about the men any of us marry, and what happens to them...if they stay in town...past their thirty-third birthday."

The curse. The one she mentioned in the letter? "You sent Daddy away because of a curse?"

Mama's eyes meet mine, sad and angry at the same time. "Yes," she says simply, rising to her feet. "It was the only way to save him."

Chapter Eighteen

✿❀❁

"Save him from what?" the horror in my voice echoes in the room. Mama glances around and makes a shushing noise.

Her gaze once more goes to the sad little table, as though there's an answer on it. "People don't believe in this stuff." It's as though I'm not even there as she's speaking. "*I* don't believe in this stuff."

Pulling out the chair, I resume my seat, partially because my legs are trembling. "You believed it enough to send Daddy away. Now tell me what this curse is."

She drops back into her chair and swallows hard. "The Holloway women—our family—we can't escape it."

Dread bubbles up in my belly. "What does it do? How is Dad affected?"

She shakes her head slightly. "I thought it was all crazy talk, an old wives' tale, nothing more, but I couldn't take the chance, and your father"—she cracks a patient smile—"he really did always dream of performing that god-awful music of his."

"Sending him away protected him from the curse?"

"Seems to." She finally meets my eyes. "The men we marry are cursed to die at a young age. Thirty-Three. None of them make it past that from what I know."

A hard lump sticks in my throat. I think of Uncle Sadler and the grandfather I never met because he was dead before Mama and Aunt Willa hit their teens. I search my brain for others and realize I can't remember any men in the family making it to old age. "All of them?"

Mama turns stoic. "As far back as I can remember, although it's said several of the Holloway women managed to circumvent the curse to some degree to keep their partners safe."

"How? Like...divorcing them?"

"If the men leave this town, or weren't born here, they stand a chance."

"This is for real?" At her nod, I blow out a long breath and sit back in the chair, the implications drowning me. "And you were going to tell me this when? I showed you that letter and you said Aunt Willa was crazy, and all this time you knew about the curse."

Her eyes close briefly before she resets her face and opens them. Determination darkens her pupils. "There's a lot about our family that isn't normal, or accepted, in this town. I was trying to protect you. Protect our family reputation."

I don't doubt that, but I'm still angry that she kept this from me. I'm not sure I've ever believed in curses, although I've heard of plenty of them. In the South, we run the gamut between believing in Voodoo, Hoodoo, and Santeria, all the way up to being sinners bound for hell in our more mainstream religions. "Who put this curse on us?"

She rings her hands, glancing back over her shoulder toward the door. "Do you remember the history of the town?"

"What they taught us in school, sure."

In the distance, we hear the sound of the bell over the entry door. Mabel Shackleford sticks her head inside the room again. "I am *so* sorry to bother you again, Mayor, but we're going to need this room. I do hope you understand."

As Mama and I rise, she says, "I really have to get to the office. Let's discuss this later, okay?"

It's not okay, but as I follow her out, passing Timmy on the ladder still struggling with hanging the picture, I feel slightly relieved that we had this much of a breakthrough. I'm afraid at the same time, thanks to whatever this curse is.

I want to call my father, make sure he's okay. I want to help Timmy, but have no idea how to get him to cross over. I want to find out who put this hex on my family and get that sucker broken, posthaste.

Mama and I pass a large group of Barbara's family members filing into the parlor. Mama greets each of them, shaking hands and offering condolences.

Outside, the air is crisp, the sun bright, though lacking heat. I shiver as I wait for her. Earlier, I sent Winter pictures of the contents of the trunk, including a couple from the ledger. Checking my phone, I see her reply.

Your aunt was a tough cookie. She was definitely offering services for pay that involved the dead.

Great, I think, a fresh shiver raising goosebumps on my skin.

The message goes on. *The food names are a code, probably people you know right there in town. You should check out this Thorny Toad place, ask some questions. Someone there will know.*

Wait until I tell her about the curse.

Mama bursts through the glass doors into the sunshine already pulling her phone from her handbag. A clear ringing emits from it and sets my already jumpy nerves on edge. "Do not answer that," I tell her.

For once, she listens, glancing between me and the screen before lowering the phone to her side and pressing her lips together. "Tonight," she says. "I promise. Tonight, we'll talk about what's going on."

I heave a sigh as she hustles to her car, leaving me with more questions and a terrible sense of foreboding.

Chapter Nineteen

❧❦❧

When I arrive back at Aunt Willa's the sun is shining and the temperature rising. I find Logan helping Mr. Uphill with bed and breakfast visitors arriving for the fall festival.

"Are you a bellhop, too?" I call as I walk up the path.

Logan looks up from unloading suitcases from the elderly women's trunk in the driveway. "Nah, Davie called off sick." He smiles, looking me over from head to toe. "Hey, you look nice today."

In other words, based on the teasing note in his voice, I'm wearing street clothes rather than my sleepwear for once. "Thought I'd shock the world today and act normal."

He gives a half-hearted laugh, dappled sunlight playing on his hair. "I sort of like your quirkiness. You're…unique."

Heat rushes to my cheeks. Stumped for a reply, I look away, seeing Mr. Uphill fly down the front steps to greet his guest. As he assists the woman onto the porch, he glances at me and waves. "Hello, Ava."

I return the wave. Preston Uphill, tall, gangly, and a complete nerd, is the well-known resident Thornhollow historian. He's a dyed-in-the-wool bachelor, who seems to enjoy taking care of others.

"Thank you for letting us use your fridge and freezer space," I call to him. "Please help yourself to that food if you need it for this weekend's rush. Just don't tell the auxiliary gals, okay?"

He assists the woman inside before he strolls over to the fence, giving me a warm smile. "That's kind of you. How are you feeling today?" He points toward the back of my head.

I touch the lump there, somewhat smaller now. "Better, thank you." Logan disappears inside with the luggage, and I stare up at Mr. Uphill's wrinkled face and wonder how old he is. He's seemed ancient since I was a girl, although he hasn't truly aged substantially in all these years. "Say, do you know anything about my family's connection to Tabitha Holloway? I mean, I know we're descendants and all, but I wondered if there was information you could tell me about her specifically. What was she like?"

Curiosity fires behind his gray eyes, but he's nothing if not polite and doesn't ask why I want to know. "I've written a whole section on her in *The History of Thornhollow, Volume 1*. There's a copy of the book at the historical society library. Would you like to look at it? I'm president, you know, so I can get you in later today before the public hours."

The historical society exists in an old gothic house off Main Street, donated to the town by Uphill's great-grandfather. It houses antiques, paintings, and various maps, newspapers, and other oddities about the town and area.

"Shoot, my afternoon is full." Behind me, I hear muffled noises and glance over my shoulder to see Tabitha scratching at the display window glass from inside.

Logan joins us, his gaze drifting to the window as well. The cat's lips are pulled back, and her gaze is fierce on us.

I turn back to Mr. Uphill. "What I'm most interested in is if Tabitha had any enemies."

The man's curiosity becomes more apparent and he tilts his head. "Tabitha and Samuel were run out of Colonial Williamsburg for their non-Puritan beliefs, you know. I would assume they both had plenty of enemies."

Logan's gaze shifts to Mr. Uphill. "Non-Puritan?"

Mr. Uphill continues to look at me as he answers Logan. "Tabitha was an *herbalist*"—he makes air quotes—"and what some labeled a mystic. Basically, she was a witch. She claimed to be able to see the future." He does an eyeroll that would give Mama a run for her money. "Samuel was nothing but a constable, a married man, seemingly respectable until she showed up. Tabitha broke up his marriage and he left town with her to come here. Quite scandalous. They stayed amongst a tribe of natives in the hills north of here...not far from your winery." This he directs to Logan before returning his attention to me. "That was before they officially founded the town in 1703."

The date sticks in my memory from history class, but I've never heard these details about Sam and Tabby having an affair. "I didn't know Samuel had been married before."

Mr. Uphill makes a noise in the back of his throat as if I've said a bad joke. "Yes, well, while those who came later insisted Samuel and Tabitha were married, there are no records to that effect. Tabitha bewitched Samuel and that's why he left a successful career and a loving wife. Of course, others insist the two acted heroically, if you can believe it, keeping the original town laws simple—no rum, no slaves, and no lawyers. And folks could worship as they pleased."

"No lawyers?" Logan says with mock horror.

I smirk at his sour face. "Sounds like a good law to me."

He shoots me a glare, but then reluctantly smiles.

Dang, I hate myself for thinking he may have anything to do with the missing bank documents.

Mr. Uphill checks his watch. "I'm packed to the rafters for the weekend. I'm going to be sleeping on a cot in the kitchen to accommodate everyone. I hate to break off, but I need a clone to get everything done at this point."

"We can chat later. Don't overdo it." I secretly hope that he does use the food the auxiliary delivered. "I saw you working in your garden late last night. I know you have a lot to take care of, but you need rest, too."

Halfway to the drive, he stops and turns back. "You saw me...?"

I hear another flurry of Tabitha attacking the window and glance at her. What is her problem? Arthur and Lancelot have joined her, though they sit as still as sphinxes. I ignore them. "If you need gardening done for the big weekend festival, I'm sure Brax or Logan can help."

Mr. Uphill's jaw twitches. "Yes, well, it's all done for now. I simply couldn't sleep last night worrying about details for this weekend. Working with the soil and flowers relaxes me."

Aunt Willa used to claim the same thing. "You didn't happen to see or hear anything down by the creek the night my aunt died, did you?"

I glance at Logan to watch his reaction, but he's frowning at the cats in the window.

Mr. Uphill's eyes sadden. "Unfortunately, I was holed up in my office, prepping for this weekend. Detective Jones mentioned there might have been a prowler that evening, but I never even looked out my window. Last-minute schedule changes, some reservations, ordering extra food and supplies, you know how it is."

"Of course. Thanks, anyway," I offer, and he nods his goodbye.

Logan deftly jumps the wrought iron fence between us, which is a sight since he's in dress slacks and a tie. But he hasn't lost his athleticism since high school and he lands easily on his feet. He brushes his hands together, wiping off dirt. "What's up with the history lesson, Fantome?"

I glance at the street as a champagne-colored SUV worth more than a year of my wages slides up in front of the law office. "Just something Mama mentioned today that made me curious about my ancestor." I switch gears, once more watching him closely. "By the way, Rosie told me you were here and you spoke to my aunt in private the day she died."

He nods. "We spoke often. I am—was—her lawyer."

"What did you talk about?"

He rubs his hands together again. "She told me you were coming home, and that you'd be upset about the house."

"She was right. Anything else?"

A glance at the SUV. "Nothing I can tell you about presently. When we go over her last will and testament, I think you'll get some answers to your questions."

Avoidance or does he truly believe that? "Fine. Are you familiar with the Thorny Toad?"

He straightens his tie. "Sure. It's outside city proper, south of town. The old Guillen Metal Works building near the train tracks, you know the one?"

At my nod, he continues, "Guillen went out of business and sold the building to somebody who doesn't live around here. They rented it out, and a couple of...um, folks, decided to put in a bar and grill. I hear the patrons are into a lot of woo-woo stuff."

I know what he means, but I'm curious to hear his explanation. "Woo-woo?"

He heads for the sidewalk. "You know, psychic stuff. Metaphysical, new age, whatever you call it." A woman gets out of the SUV and waves at him. He waves back. "Gotta run. Mom wants to go to lunch and review the details of the tour on Sunday. You should come with us."

I'm not ready to take on his mother or discuss the tour yet. "I have an appointment to handle, but thanks."

He walks backward down the path, giving me another grin. "See you at parade practice this afternoon?"

For some silly reason, I can't stop from grinning back. "I'll be there."

His smile grows wider as he turns to jog away, using the gate to leave the property rather than jumping the fence this time. His mother gives me a nod before climbing into the passenger side, letting her son take the wheel.

My phone rings and I dig it out of my purse "Hello?"

Rosie's voice raises the hair on the back of my neck. "Ava? Oh thank God. You have to come quick."

"Where are you?"

"I'm at the country club. With Miranda."

The grin falls off my face, dread forming in my belly. "What's wrong?"

"Everything," she wails. Panic fills the connection. "All hell just broke loose, and I think I'm gonna have to send our bride to the hospital."

Chapter Twenty

❦

The Thornhollow Country Club is a bastion of Southern glory and prestige. As I drive through the front gates, passing rolling greens and golfers squeezing in eighteen holes before winter, I wonder what Sam and Tabitha would think of the formal plantation house that rises like a beacon half a mile away.

More importantly, I wonder with a sense of trepidation why the ambulance is parked out front.

After pulling into a visitor's slot, I make my way to the scene. Miranda is surrounded by Reverend Stout and Wesley, the country club manager, and several others. She's holding an oxygen mask to her face, her porcelain skin paler than normal, and in between deep breaths she's yelling at those gathered. "Why is this *happening?*"

Everyone in Thornhollow loves a good drama, so I'm not surprised when a trio of female golfers eagerly exit the building and join the onlookers. They exchange comments and sly smiles behind their hands, and I'm sure what unfolds will be town gossip before the sun goes down. One of the women happens to be Priscilla Barnes, and I grind my teeth as I march forward.

Lucky for Prissy, Rosie stops me before I can engage her. "Thank the Blessed Mother you're here. Miranda is pitching a hissy fit."

Fern peaks her tiny head over the edge of Rosie's tote and blinks her eyes at me. I can see she's trembling. Rosie draws me away from the crowd, Prissy narrowing her eyes as we pass by her clique. "What happened?" I ask under my breath.

"I came to check on the electrical issues—which, by the way, Dale Ingram said are non-existent—and Miranda showed up. The minute she walked in things went wonky."

Things have been wonky, in my opinion, since my aunt died. "Describe 'wonky.'"

"Well, a giant vase of flowers in the vestibule exploded when she walked past it. Flowers, water, glass went everywhere! The lights started flickering, sending Dale off to investigate again. Then everyone's cellphones started going off, even those with their ringers silenced like mine. It was so crazy. I'm telling you, Ava, it was the weirdest thing I've ever seen!"

"Is everyone all right?"

She nods, blowing out a breath through her lips, "Everyone but poor Miranda."

We both look over at Reverend Stout, encouraging our bride to stop talking and focus on breathing. His gentle voice coaxes and soothes. "It's gonna be all right now, Miss Miranda. You'll see. This is all just probably something silly, like Mercury retrograde or something."

Instead of calming Miranda, this statement sends a fresh wave of panic through her. She frantically scans the crowd and sees Rosie and me a few feet away. "Is it Mercury retrograde?" she yells. "Why didn't anyone tell me? I can't get married during a retrograde! I'm doomed!"

Fern whimpers and disappears inside the tote. The fact that anyone in my hometown actually knows what a Mercury retrograde is surprises me. Good thing I've had experience with panicked brides. It's quite common that when the countdown to the wedding is under five days they turn into she-devils or complete basket cases.

Calling up my professional face and confident manner, I brush past the others and take Miranda's hand. "It's not Mercury retrograde, and everything is going to be perfectly fine, like Reverend Stout said." I pray I'm right on both counts. "Breathe, Miranda. That's it. I'm here and I'm going to take good care of you, like my Aunt Willa would. You *will* have the wedding of your dreams, I promise."

She flings her arms around my neck, breaking out in relieved sobs. I pat her back to calm her, and over her shoulder I see the champagne-colored SUV with Logan and his mother approaching the parking lot.

As I continue to pat Miranda, Prissy makes her way to us. "Last chance, Miranda. Let me take over and provide you with a wedding you deserve."

I curl my lip at Prissy over Miranda's shoulder, and she has the nerve to smile. I set Miranda back slightly, keeping my hands on her arms. "Well, there's the problem," I tell her, cool and collected. "Prissy's here."

Miranda turns her head, eyes puffy and nose red, and it only takes a second for the seed I planted yesterday to bloom. "You *are* jinxed!" She points an accusatory finger at Prissy. "*You're* the reason all this is happening."

Prissy rears back, as if slapped. The women in her clique looked stunned then snicker behind their hands. I sense Logan and his mother on the outskirts of the group and know it's time to wrap this scene up.

"Now, now, ladies," Reverend Stout mollifies us. "Let's get Miranda to the clinic and make sure she's okay."

He guides her to the waiting ambulance, but her gaze stays on Prissy. "You stay away from me and Ty, you hear? I will *not* allow you to ruin our big day!"

The reverend gets her up the steps and inside the ambulance, closing the door, as Wesley runs around to jump in the front. Prissy, hands on hips, whirls on me. "How dare you besmirch my reputation in town!"

When Prissy's mad, she's meaner than a wet cat. All eyes are on me, so I keep my smile in place, refusing to give her an ounce of satisfaction. I lean toward her, lowering my voice. "Aunt Willa always said if you can't run with the big dogs, you better stand under the porch. Why don't you go back to your golf game and leave event planning to me?"

She calls me a nasty name. "If anyone's jinxed in this town, it's you and your no-good family."

Several people suck in a collective breath. I turn to the country club manager—his gold name tag, glinting in the sun, reads Dirk. "May I speak to you privately inside?"

Nervously, he nods. "Yes, of course." He holds out a hand to usher me toward the entrance. As we climb the wide steps of the terrace, he glances back at the ambulance pulling away. I can see in his face, and his anxious movements, he's afraid Miranda might sue the place.

Rosie and several of the gawkers follow us. "I don't understand this at all," Dirk tells me. "We've never had issues like this."

Entering the cool foyer, I see one of the day workers placing a fresh fall centerpiece on the side table where I'm guessing the flowers used to be before the vase exploded.

"I'm sure there's a reasonable explanation," I assure him. "Is it possible Miranda accidentally knocked into the flowers on the stand? Or that the electrical junction box is overloaded? Perhaps a sudden increase in EMF knocked out the electricity or caused the phones to act erratically?"

"What happened?" Logan inserts himself at my side, startling me. His mother gives me a nod as she, too, joins us.

Before Dirk can reply, Rosie jumps in to give them the rundown. As she does, I hear a woman's laugh behind us. Turning, I see no one. The crowd has returned to golf games and gossip. Not even Prissy is in sight.

Something tickles the back of my neck then tugs a strand of my hair, "Ow!" Grasping my hair, I scan for the culprit.

All eyes land on me at the outburst. "You okay?" Logan askes.

With a sinking feeling, I nod, but continue to scan the area.

Dirk gestures to the overhead light. "Everything seems fine now. Perhaps you'd like to see the ballroom and go over the reception details, Ms. Fantome?"

I understand his need to right this ship, and I'm onboard. "Great idea." I see the fake flowers on the table wobble, and hurriedly I step up to put out a hand to steady them. It passes through a cold spot that raises goosebumps on my skin.

Mrs. Cross unbuttons her expensive tweed jacket, her perfect hair and makeup creating the illusion she's much younger. "Ava, I need to speak with you as well, about the wine tour."

"Why don't you have lunch with us," Logan reiterates, putting me on the spot. "When you're done with the reception details, come find us in the dining room."

His mother looks slightly displeased, and I consider begging off since I have no idea what Aunt Willa planned for the tour, but it would get one thing checked off my list. "Maybe just for a glass of tea, and then I'll leave you two to your lunch."

In the ballroom, Rosie, Dirk and I review the decorations, the menu, the DJ setup, and the itinerary of the wedding and reception. Several times, as Dirk and Rosie walk me through the evening's timeline, I feel a breeze on my neck or hear an invisible someone comment with, "No way," or "Never gonna happen."

This disembodied voice sends worry threading through me. We have a ghost and if she's as strong as I think she is, she could very well ruin Miranda's evening.

I look at the others. "Can I have a minute alone?"

Dirk and Rosie give me odd looks but nod and walk out together.

Once the door closes behind them, I speak to the ghost. "Okay, listen. I'm having a *really* bad week, and whoever you are, just tell me why you're doing this so I can help you."

Silence is the reply.

Frustrated, I spin in a circle. "Now you're clamming up? What are you, chicken?"

Without warning, a frosty puff of air slides down my spine. "I'm Calista Lionhart," the ghost says, close enough to make me jump, "and Ty Durham is *mine*."

Chapter Twenty-One

Worst fears confirmed, I attempt to interrogate
Calista, but all she does is give my hair another
yank.

"Stop that," I chastise, using Mama's stern voice. "We have to
work this out."

Fading laughter is the only reply, and Calista disappears.

Dirk pokes his head back in, looking abashed. "Mrs. Cross
said to tell you your iced tea is getting warm."

My mother is a member of the country club and has been
since she took office ten years ago, but we were never accepted
as true members, a privilege reserved for folds like the Cross
family and their counterparts. Dirk offers to show me to the
dining room, but I wave him off.

Pulling myself together, I find Rosie and ask if she wants to
come with me to talk to Mrs. Cross, but she shakes her head
adamantly. "I prefer to stay as far away from her as I can get."

Fern peers up at me with her big eyes again and I reach out
to scratch under her chin. "Are you throwing me to the wolves
when I'm doing all I can to help?" I tease with a hint of truth.

She gives me a wicked smile. "From what I've seen, you can

handle her just fine. I'll check on Miranda and get back to the Chapel for our meeting with Penny at three."

"Did you ever know a woman named Calista Lionhart?"

She screws up her face as if tasting something sour. "I didn't know her personally, but a tragic story to be sure." She lowers her voice as a couple goes past us on their way to the greens. "She and Ty Durham were a couple in high school. One night, they were out partying and ended up in a car accident. Ty survived, she didn't."

"Who's fault was it? The accident?"

Another face from Rosie. "There were contradictory stories —the police believed Calista was driving. Ty said he was, and that Calista pulled him from the wreck before she died. His parents put the kibosh on him confessing to driving, though, and eventually the story that she was in the driver's seat is the one that stuck. Whatever happened, she did save his life. The car caught fire after she pulled him from the wreck. She died lying next to him from internal injuries."

At least now I understand why our ghost is hanging around —unfinished business. She may not realize she's dead, or believes Ty owes her for surviving while she didn't.

As Rosie leaves, I wonder how I'm going to handle Calista and her poltergeist activities. Whatever happens, I have to make sure Miranda's wedding goes off without a hitch.

In the dining room, Logan and his mother are deep in conversation over their lunches, but his gaze zeroes in on me the moment I step to the hostess station. He waves me over and comes to his feet to pull out a chair for me.

I thank him and sit, nodding at Mrs. Cross as I wipe moisture from the glass of tea waiting for me. "With everything going on, I'm afraid I haven't had a chance to go over the details of the tour with Rosie yet, but I assure you, I'll dig into them tonight. Is there anything in particular you're concerned about?"

She dabs her mouth carefully with the cloth napkin. "First, let me extend my sympathies over your aunt." She sends a pointed look in Logan's direction, and he gives her a nearly imperceptible nod. "I don't know where my manners were earlier. The commotion outside made them fly right out of my head."

The smile she gives me is forced, as if admitting any error on her part goes against everything in her body. Did Logan reprimand her for not offering her sympathies? Interesting.

"I certainly appreciate that." I take a big sip of tea, realizing I'm tense—not because a barracuda of the Thornhollow upper echelon has me in her sights, but because I'm waiting for Calista to make another appearance. "Aunt Willa's passing was quite a shock."

"You *are* up to handling the Pumpkins and Peach Wine event, aren't you?" Her blue eyes are sharp and calculating. "If not, I need to know right now. The event is the biggest profit-maker and marketing promotion of the year for us."

Logan clears his throat, "Mother doesn't mean to sound insensitive. We know this is a terrible burden to place on you, along with taking over Miranda's wedding when you're in mourning. It's just that—"

I raise a hand to stop him. "No apology necessary. I understand. The event is critical to the town's tourism dollars, as well as your business. I'm sure Aunt Willa would want me to fulfil her duties and make sure it goes off without a hitch."

This seems to relieve both of them. Mrs. Cross smiles, and it comes closer to being genuine this time. "I admired your aunt. She had a real nose for business."

This revelation shocks me, and some of the feelings I have for the barracuda morph into appreciation. "That really does mean a lot to me."

We get down to business and she tells me exactly what she and Aunt Willa had planned for the winery's part of the tour.

Honestly, this open house style of event sounds like a piece of cake compared to pulling off the Burnett-Durham wedding. I've planned events here and there, and with Rosie's help we should be fine.

Logan offers to order dessert for all of us, but I'm eager to leave and call Winter and dig up the courage to look at the hiding place in the armoire my aunt mentioned. I need to find out more about the curse, check on Miranda, and dive into double-checking the hundreds of minute details for the tour on Sunday.

I also need to interrogate Tabitha's reaction to Mr. Uphill and Logan earlier, and figure out a way to force the marmalade cat to talk to me. "Dessert sounds lovely, but I really must be going. And unfortunately for my waistband, I've already had too many delicious desserts in the past twenty-four hours, thanks to the ladies' auxiliary."

When Logan rises and offers to walk me out, I feel a cold breeze run over my arm and instantly beg off saying I'm going to the restroom and I'll see him at the parade practice.

I do head to the restroom, whispering Calista's name here and there, while trying not to attract attention from those coming and going in the halls.

The smell of honeysuckle wafts through the immaculate sitting room that's part of the restroom, separated from the sinks and stalls and offering seated spots to fix your makeup and chat. This place is nicer than pretty much any home I've ever lived in, complete with fancy folded towels and designer soaps. Even the wallpaper screams money.

At a loss on how to handle Calista—or pretty much any of the other things on my spirit to-do list, I send Winter an SOS. *Need to know about breaking curses, and what to do about a poltergeist who died saving the guy she loved and doesn't want him to get married.*

This is the busiest season of the year for the Whitethorne

sisters, and I feel guilty for adding to Winter's stress with my drama, but who else can I ask?

I pace, waiting for a reply. "Last chance, Calista," I call to the empty restroom. "If you want my help, you need to talk to me. You're a ghost, in case you didn't realize it, and you need to cross over to the other side. Heaven. Trying to stop Ty's wedding to Miranda won't work, not as long as I'm here. You can never be with him again." *At least not until he dies*, I think morbidly. "Do you really want him to spend the rest of his life pining over you? Don't you want him to be happy?"

Silence again meets my ears. Frustrated, I want to throw one of the soaps against the wall. Definitely not proper manners.

"Calista, please, talk to me. Let me help you."

She makes it clear she doesn't want my help when all four toilets erupt in geysers of water.

Chapter Twenty-Two

Penelope Calhoun is as opposite of Miranda Burnett as you can get, even if you disregard her multiple tattoos and piercings.

When I arrive at Aunt Willa's a good hour before her appointment, I'm a little wet and a lot pissed off. Shower-by-toilet is not a fun experience.

Rosie shows shock at my appearances and asks what happened. She gasps when I tell her, and because I'm angry, wet, and frustrated, I slip and mention Calista's involvement. She doesn't even blink at the ghost story.

"You have the gift," she says unfazed. "Willa always claimed you did."

"You knew she could talk to ghosts?"

"Half the town knows, but they're way too uncomfortable about that kind of thing. Easier to pretend it was nothing but gossip. Willa worked hard at gaining everyone's trust to put them at ease."

"Do you know anything about the Thorny Toad?"

Again, she's unfazed. "Oh sure. My *abuela* does readings there on Saturday nights sometimes. Miss Willa went once a month or so, if she didn't have a wedding, and helped a lot of people."

"Helped them with what exactly?"

"Bringing them peace and some closure after their loved ones passed."

I think on this as I stumble upstairs and shuck my clothes. I take a long hot shower, as if I can wash away the country club disaster as well as my worries and doubts about all of this.

When the water runs cold, I towel myself off and find Tabby sitting near the hamper. Her gold eyes look bored. Or haughty maybe. Hard to tell which.

"Tabitha, I need your help." I dress quickly, feeling a bit weird about her watching me. "I know you can speak. Tell me what's going on. Did someone really kill Aunt Willa? If so, who? And can you really shapeshift? Why did you react so weird this morning over Mr. Uphill? Or was it Logan?"

Please don't let be Logan.

She rises slowly to her feet, stretches and arches her back. Then she strolls away.

Darn cat. Looks like bribery is next, and I best check for something worthy to do it with.

My phone shows a reply text from Winter. *"Curses are nothing to play around with,"* it says. *"There are herbs, salts, crystals, and talismans that can break and keep the curse broken. As far as the poltergeist? Just as tricky. Let's talk later, I need more details."*

So do I, I think to myself.

I text back, *"After I talk to Mama, I'll call you."*

Bracing myself, I head to Aunt Willa's room and stand in front of her antique armoire. At least I think it's an antique, but maybe Uncle Saddler made it. It's possible he put the secret compartment in it under her guidance. "Aunt Willa?" I call softly. "Are you here? Any possibility we can talk?"

There's no response. Downstairs, Rosie is singing to some music she's playing. Tabby is nowhere to be found, Arthur and

Lancelot are probably still in the front windows, napping like they were when I first came in.

Reaching out, I toy with the knobs on the front of the armoire then run a hand along the top edge of the cabinet. It's beautiful craftsmanship and I smell a faint scent of Aunt Willa's favorite perfume...a simple lilac and vanilla mixture.

"You know, I've done everything you asked." I shift around to the side of the armoire. "I came home, I told Mama your preferences for the funeral, I'm looking into the curse, and I'm taking care of your brides. I'm even filling in for you at the parade. I went through the trunk, and now I'm ready to see whatever you have hidden in this armoire. All I've come up with in return are more questions. I sure could use you or Tabby to answer some of them."

The doorbell goes off downstairs and I hear Rosie answering. "Oh, you're early."

A raspy voice answers, "Am I? I thought my appointment was at two."

It's twenty after, and I should rush down and help Rosie out. Instead, I decide it's now or never. I can take a quick peek inside the armoire then run downstairs to handle this appointment.

As if she's read my mind, Rosie calls up the stairs. "I've got this, Ava. Take your time."

Of course, she'd give me a way out, but, no, if I'm taking over the business, even if it's just for the weekend, I'm going to be present during Penny's appointment.

Pushing on the side panel, I flinch slightly when it pops open half an inch. "Curiouser and curiouser," I murmur, quoting from *Alice in Wonderland*. That's what I feel like right now—that I've somehow fallen down a rabbit hole and I can't find my way out of this upside-down world.

My gaze scans the contents inside the hidden compartment. Dried herbs, small drawstring bags, tapered candles, and other tiny items hang from a multitude of gold hooks. My brain can't quite find the connection between all of them, but they suggest some witchy-ness has been going on. I've been in Winter's store, Conjure, and recognize the ingredients for spells.

This sets me back a bit. Between the items logged in the ledger and this, it suggests Aunt Willa was a witch, along with being a medium. Like Tabitha, I think, remembering Mr. Uphill's story.

Again, Winter is my expert in that area, so I take pictures and send them to her before I head downstairs.

Rosie introduces me to Penelope, who insists I call her Penn. She seems genuinely upset about Aunt Willa's death and gives me a hug.

Her cut-off shorts and tank top put her multitude of tattoos on display and I wonder if she's at all chilly, although she doesn't show it. Thick wool socks poke out of the top of her black motorcycle boots, and she has enough silver piercings, I'm almost blinded each time they catch the light as she speaks. "I totally understand if you decide to close the business and not do my wedding."

The rasp in her voice sounds like she spent last night screaming at a concert, but I suspect it's normal for her. I don't remember her from my years growing up here. I motion her back into her seat, seeing a female ghost hovering around out of the corner of my eye. "Of course I'm going to handle your wedding. Rosie has everything under control." I may not, but she does. I try to catch better sight of the ghost connected to this client, but it disappears each time I shift my gaze. "Tell me about the groom."

The next hour flies by, Penn lighting up as she talks about Beau John Reed—known as BJ—and how they met. Both are transplants to Thornhollow, and she tells me how he proposed on a trip to the Badlands, and the fact she never thought she'd say "I do."

"I'm sort of a non-conformist," she tells me with a chuckle.

I pretend surprise. "Never would have guessed."

The fact the two of them are holding their reception at the Thorny Toad piques my interest. She and Rosie fill me in about the details—big place, plenty of seating, the manager, Rhys— who happens to be Brax's partner—has happily okayed it.

I shift my gaze to Rosie. "Braxton LaFleur?"

"The one and only. You didn't know? He and Rhys have been a thing for a while now."

"I know *that*." I rub my forehead. "I mean about them running the Toad."

"Oh." Rosie gives a shrug. "Rhys loves the metaphysical stuff and he's a talented drink maker. It was a natural fit."

"Rhys reads palms," Penn adds. She turns one of her hands up. "He looked at my heart line, or whatever it's called, and told me I was destined to meet my soul mate. Two days later, *bam*. BJ came into my life and we've been together ever since."

More things I never knew. I make a mental note to chastise Brax later. I don't understand why he never mentioned to me that Rhys had his own business.

The appointment comes to an end half an hour later. Penn is hugging me goodbye when the front door opens and one of my favorite people in the whole world hustles in, carrying two tote bags with *Beehive Diner* stamped on them.

Queenie sets them on the floor and throws open her generously sized arms to me. "Come here, baby girl."

The rush of relief I feel at seeing her is overwhelming. She was a second mother to me growing up, right alongside my aunt.

I rush to her and let her strong arms crush me in a bear hug.

Chapter Twenty-Three

Queenie and I both erupt in conversation, barely drawing breath between questions and answers.

Rosie sees Penn out, her ghost friend leaving with her, and Queenie hustles me into the kitchen.

There, she sits me down at the table and begins unloading the bags, some of my favorite foods being set before me. Chicken and dumplings, biscuits, chocolate pie. My mouth waters.

She wants to know everything that's happened since I've come home, apologizing for not coming to see me sooner. "Brax said the ladies' auxiliary was here yesterday, and that you were sleeping through most of it, so I didn't want to bother you."

Queenie avoids the auxiliary as much as possible. "I'm just glad you're here now. There's so much going on, and I'm dog-paddling trying to stay afloat."

"Talk to me, baby girl."

She knows all, and I don't have any secrets from her for the most part. I start with Aunt Willa's letter, showing it to her and watching her pull on her glasses to read it. When she finishes, I tell her succinctly about most of the stuff that's happened since that letter, and she motions at me to eat.

I do, and she checks the back of my head, to make sure the lump is better. Satisfied, she returns to her seat. "What did you see when you died?"

"Nothing." I swallow a dumpling. "I don't really think I died, though."

She clucks under her breath, letting me know she disagrees. "Don't you think that may be the cause of all this…increased awareness you have?"

She means about the ghosts. I chew and nod, but ask, "Couldn't a concussion cause it?"

Another cluck. "You really believe Willa Rae was murdered?"

They were close, and I find myself trying to reassure her. "There's no evidence, so maybe not. I'm confused about so much right now. I don't want to *not* look into it and then have unanswered questions after she's buried."

This garners a nod of approval. "What else? You're not telling me everything, I can see it in your eyes."

I debate telling her about Tabitha, and the inanimate objects speaking to me. I sip tea, eat more food to buy time. This makes her happy, even though she knows what I'm doing. "The ghosts are freaking me out, that's all," I finally admit.

"I'm certainly glad to see you embracing your gift with the spirit world," she says, shoving another biscuit at me.

This is Queenie—food equals love. I'm already stuffed, but I break a piece of the biscuit off, letting the buttery beauty of it melt on my tongue before I answer. "Is it really a gift, Queenie?"

There are three women in my life that I couldn't do without, and she is one of them. She and Aunt Willa were always close, and even though they grew up in very different types of families, they were the best of friends. I've always wondered if they weren't as much sisters as Mama and Willa were. Heart bonds can be as strong as those by blood.

Queenie leans close, her beautiful dark eyes searching mine. "Don't you go talking like that now. It *is* a gift, and you have to stop denying it."

I ask her if she knows about the curse on our family, and she straightens, glancing away. "We never talked much about it, but your aunt believed it was a real thing."

"I have to tackle that after I get through the Burnett-Durham wedding."

The subject switches to the big event, and I fill her in on my bride who's about to have a nervous breakdown, and about a poltergeist who's trying to stop the wedding entirely.

She sits back in her seat, laughing out loud. Her boisterous laugh makes me smile as it echoes off the high ceiling. "Lawd, you've got yourself a handful there."

I quiz her if she knows how to handle such a thing and she tells me to talk to Brax. He can set me up with somebody from the Thorny Toad who can help me deal with it.

I tell her about Winter and my hope that she can help guide me.

Talk turns to her business when I ask her how things are going. Like my aunt, Queenie loves what she does and it shows. She becomes very animated as she tells me about her new menu, the expansion she's thinking about doing next year, and how her catering business is just getting its legs under it. I'm proud of her, and I feel like I could burst sharing in the joy of her success.

She checks the watch on her arm and makes a little squeaking sound as she jumps up. "We gotta go, or we're going to be late."

We leave the dirty dishes in the sink, and drive her SUV over to the municipal parking lot that adjoins Reverend Stout's church. Rosie claims she'll be over in a bit. People are just starting to pull in, excitement in the air, as the practice gets under way.

Queenie sets up a long folding table and pulls out plastic containers full of cookies, breads, and muffins. The sugar cookies are in the shape of fall leaves and pumpkins, and I snitch one as I lay out individually wrapped slices of pumpkin bread and her famous cinnamon apple cake.

As she gets out coolers of water, sweet tea, and warm cider, I line up cider muffins and a selection of her new candy items. Logan arrives and comes to see us. He buys a cider and asks Queenie if she has any of her hot cinnamon candies.

"Brought some just for you, Mr. Lawyer," she says, digging around in the back of the SUV and bringing out a box with more candy in it. She hands him a bag of bright red candies. "Logan is one of my best taste testers," she tells me.

He eats a handful and a look of pure heaven comes over his face. "Queenie, you're going to give Ty Durham's family a run for their money in the candy department."

I freeze, remembering the entry in Aunt Willa's ledger about Candy Lane—could it be Ty, or someone in his family, that Aunt Willa helped?

More and more people pull in. Several pickup trucks with hay racks, a few antique cars, and the high school band arrive. We become busy, and Queenie's coffers start to fill as everyone wants a cookie or a piece of her famous bread. People seem happy to see me, and most have something nice to say about my aunt. I find myself smiling and laughing and generally enjoying the atmosphere.

When there's a lull in activity, Logan, who's been chatting it up with various council members, sneaks up behind me and taps me on the shoulder. When I face him, he holds out the bag of hot cinnamons. "You've got to try these."

"Oh, thanks, but I'm not really into hot stuff."

A silly grin tugs at the corner of his mouth. "Funny, I was thinking you needed a little more spice in your life."

His eyes are so blue, and that smile…

Everything I'm worried about flies out of my head. The sun is sinking, shooting beautiful peachy rays of light over our portion of the parking lot. He jiggles the candies in the bag between us, "Come on, Ava, take a risk. Try a candy."

I waver.

He sees it. "I've never known you to chicken out of a challenge."

A spark of competition usually reserved for Prissy Barnes ignites. Holding out my hand, I accept one of the tiny red candies from him and pop it in my mouth.

The taste of cinnamon explodes in my mouth, a sharp tang of heat hitting the back of my throat. It's as if the rest of the group around us disappears, and it's only Logan and me.

"What do you think?" he asks.

I think I'm still falling down that rabbit hole. I start to answer then accidentally suck the cinnamon down my throat.

Oh ack! I gag, I cough, and then I whirl away, embarrassment hitting my cheeks. The candy is stuck, my throat on fire.

"Are you okay?" Logan asks.

My face flames anew with self-consciousness, and I try to answer, resulting in a fresh coughing attack.

Logan gently whacks me on the back. Miracle of miracles, the stuck candy dislodges and flies out of my mouth. It hits the ground, and I continue to cough raggedly, my throat spasming.

A group of gawkers has gathered. Queenie hands me a cup of water, but attempting to drink only makes the coughing worse.

I walk away, trying to get away from Logan, but he follows.

Tears run from my eyes, and he continues to gently pat me between the shoulder blades. As the worst subsides, his pats become a gentle rub, and I feel a different kind of heat flood my face.

Get it together, Ava! I can handle just about anything, but some cute guy with blue eyes offers me a piece of candy and I become a hot mess.

I hesitantly sip some water and try not to look at him, and he's polite enough to close the bag of candies and put them away inside his jacket. "What exactly happened at the country club today? Were you in the restroom when those toilets exploded?"

Great, we're going from one embarrassing situation to another. There's no way I'm going to tell him that I ended up showered in toilet water, so I wave a hand dismissively. "Already gone when it happened," I manage to get out.

Thankfully, he lets it drop, and the onlookers begin to mill around again, some giving me smiles.

We walk back over and I resume helping Queenie sell more products, speaking to a bunch of the volunteers and those in charge of the floats.

Mr. Uphill buys a cupcake and tells me he has that book for me at his place, I should come by later and get it. Walker Lee, the editor of the *Tribune*, offer's his condolences and asks me about writing up Aunt Willa's obituary. We agree to talk the next day.

Winona Redfern, who runs the thrift store, appears in a long skirt, heavy sweater, and wool scarf. Her long, wavy red hair and bright earrings blow in the gentle breeze, and she gives me a hug, along with telling me a funny story about some silverware Aunt Willa donated to the store.

Edith Warhol from the dress shop places a catering order with Queenie while I man the table. During a small rush, Logan steps in to help.

We've pretty much run out of food by the time Mama shows up, in full mayoral mode, and begins handing out maps. Her sprayed hair doesn't move in the breeze, and while she's wearing what she considers comfortable clothing, she still looks like a prominent business woman in her gray suit and a matching trench coat.

The parade goes approximately seven blocks, it's not like

people will get lost. Still, the map seems to be a popular thing, and people crowd around her to make sure they get one. Logan, next to me, watches with an amused look on his face. "Have you practiced your parade wave yet?"

I snort. "I think I can handle it."

He points in the direction of the far corner of the lot. "Did you see the sign?"

I follow where he points and see his red car, top down, shining in the last of the sun's setting rays. On the passenger side is a magnetic sign that reads "Thornhollow Grand Marshall."

"You're driving me?"

The grin makes an appearance again and I feel a slight flush rise up my cheeks. "At your service."

Sure enough, a few minutes later, Mama calls everybody to gather around and quiet down. For the next hour, she lines us up and sends us on the parade route. People come out from their businesses and homes to wave and cheer us on, even though this isn't the official event.

For the first time since I've been here, I actually feel like I'm home.

After practice I'm helping Queenie clean up and enjoying the last of the apple cider when Rosie rushes over. "Oh, Ava. What are we going to do? The ballroom at the country club is ruined!"

I set down the cider. "What?"

She swallows hard and nods. "The water flooded the entire first floor and destroyed the flooring." She heaves a shaky breath, panic in her eyes. "We can't hold the wedding there."

Her panic seeps into my own system, but I force myself to remain calm. Queenie, Logan, and several other folks in the nearby vicinity shoot distressed looks at me.

Could anything else go crazy? "Then I guess we'll move the wedding somewhere else," I state calmly.

Four hundred plus guests, two days until the wedding, how hard can that be?

Rosie steps closer, lowering her voice. "There isn't any other place else we can rent for a party of that size."

"There's gotta be," I argue.

She shakes her head, the growing twilight closing in around us. "I'm afraid Miranda and Ty have to call off the wedding."

Chapter Twenty-Four

R osie, Logan, Queenie and I gather at Aunt Willa's kitchen table. There's an assortment of food laid out, but none of us are eating.

"There has to be something," I state for the dozenth time. "If we can land the space, I can tweak the decorations and get everything back on track."

"What about the food?" Rosie asks. "The Country Club was providing a complete dinner, alcohol, the whole shebang for the reception afterward."

That is a problem. I look at Queenie. "Can you cater it?"

She sits back, her face surprised. "Honey, I'm a home cooking kinda gal, not some fancy country club chef. Besides, the wedding's in two days. I couldn't come up with enough food for that many people in such a short time."

"The country club must have already ordered the bulk of the food." I fiddle with the corner of a casserole dish. "If we could get their chef to help you create appetizers and finger food in your kitchen...?"

I leave the opportunity hanging, knowing Queenie loves a challenge.

She makes a face, but I see the wheels turning in her head. "I don't know, Ava. For you, I'd do anything, but this might be a bit of a stretch."

"It would be the absolute best advertising for the diner and your new catering business," I insist. "The country club should have all the ingredients for the food, all you'd have to do is put it together."

Frowning, she stares at me as if I've lost my mind.

"Just think about it, okay?" I beg.

She heaves a sigh, and I can see she's already thinking about recipes and dishes, her mind combing through details.

"Back to the venue." I get up and put the tea kettle on to heat. Tabitha meanders in and winds herself around my feet when I return to my seat. "Let's throw out any possibilities, no matter how crazy."

"If the weather would hold there are plenty of options." Logan ticks them off on his fingers. "You could hold the service and reception here, at the park, or in the church. You could use the church's kitchen for the food prep for the reception. The tables and DJ could all go outside in the parking lot."

"No bar at the church for the reception," Queenie offers. "The Burnetts and Durhams won't go for that."

Alcohol, everyone's got to have it.

"We can't host four hundred people here." Rosie glances around as if trying to imagine it. "The most we've done is a hundred and fifty. Colin and Lola Larimar's wedding. And that was wall to wall people. The bathroom had a constant line. It was mayhem. Fun, but... phew." She makes a dramatic face. "No way we can accommodate four hundred."

"But you could open up the yards—yours and Preston's." Logan motions toward Mr. Uphill's. "That would give you double the outdoor space and people can use my restroom at the law office, if that's an issue."

Rosie taps a well-manicured nail on the table. "Mr. Uphill

won't go for it. He's far too uptight to have that many people tramping through his backyard, and with his extra guests this weekend he won't appreciate a party with loud music going into the wee hours of the morning."

My phone rings and I don't recognize the number. I send it to voicemail. The front door opens and closes and Mama calls, "Ava?"

"In the kitchen, Mama."

She hustles in and pulls up short when she sees the gathering. "Oh, hello everyone." To me she pointedly says, "I thought we were going to talk."

Rosie's desk phone rings in the outer room and she leaves to answer it.

"We were, but I'm in crisis mode." I explain about the country club disaster. "Can you think of a venue big enough to hold four hundred people that allows alcohol and has a commercial kitchen?"

Mama's face turns pensive as she takes Rosie's chair. "That's a tall order. Let me think about it."

Rosie swings in, hanging onto the doorway. "Ava, it's Miranda."

For the next few minutes, I listen to our bride wail about the disaster. "We have to cancel," she sobs. "Ty says he doesn't care —he'll marry me anywhere, anytime, but this has to be right. This is my *dream* wedding, Ava!"

"Do not cancel. Not yet. Give me twenty-four hours. I'm going to find a place," I promise.

It takes a few minutes to convince her to go relax in a hot bath and get some sleep. Brax walks through the front door as I'm hanging up, bringing with him a waft of cold air and a look of determination. "Let's go," he says to me.

"Go where?"

"Rosie texted that you need to see the Thorny Toad. Mandy's covering for me, so I'll take you out there."

Logan appears from the kitchen. "I can drive her."

"I've got it," Brax replies, his broad chest expanding.

The two face each other and I wonder what this display is about. It's as if they're both claiming rights to me or something. "Can the Toad hold four hundred guests?" I ask.

Brax nods, not taking his gaze off Logan. "The fire chief gave us clearance for five, so shouldn't be a problem. The booth dividers for the psychics and card readers are temporary. We can fold them down and put them away in the storage room."

He finally turns his attention to me again, and I hear the jingle of Logan's keys as he pulls them from his front pocket. "More important question is," Brax says, handing me my coat. "Do you really think Ty's family will lower themselves to hold the wedding there?"

I pinch the bridge of my nose and close my eyes, Miranda's sobs ringing in my ears. "If Ty Durham really loves his fiancé, he'll convince them to do it."

Chapter Twenty-Five

The road out of town to the former metal-works building is filled with potholes and dark as the inside of a sow's belly.

Mama's car hits a rut, jarring my teeth and making the book on my lap slide into the footwell. "Sorry," she says. "I should get some of our county funds put into this road."

In the backseat, Rosie soothes Fern, who's been whining since we left. I told Brax and Logan that I needed to talk to Mama so I would be riding with her. They both insisted on following us, and Queenie volunteered to join her son in order to discuss the possibility of catering the event.

I reach for Mr. Uphill's book, a slim volume with a black cover describing the founding on our town. The penlight I'm using to read bobs as we rattle over more cracked asphalt. "You might install some lights out here, too."

Mama grips the steering wheel like a lifeline, hunching forward and attempting to avoid the worst of the holes. "I haven't been out here in a long time. I had no idea it was this bad. After the metal works closed, everyone kind of forgot about this place."

"Brax and Rhys's business is growing," Rosie tells her. "Might be time to capitalize on that and include the Thorny Toad in some of the chamber's advertising. You could draw folks from all over, I bet."

Mama snorts derisively. "To see a bunch of snake charmers?" I shoot her a glare and she shrugs in the dashboard lights. "What, you want me to believe there are legitimate psychics and card readers at this place?"

"My abuela's the real deal." Rosie's voice is firm. "Miss Willa was legitimate, too."

Mama shakes her head. "My sister—"

"Was a psychic medium," I finish for her. "And she helped a lot of people with that, as well as with other things."

"Just like Ava's doing." Rosie pats my shoulder. "Whether it's talking to people who've passed over or creating dream weddings, Ava's got the Fantome gift. She makes people happy. That's your gift, too, Miss Dixie."

Mama's ego likes that, even though she's not sure whether to argue or agree. She forces a smile in the rearview at our passenger and then slides a glance my way. "I'm not gifted in the ways Willa Rae was."

I'd wanted to open this topic with her tonight more smoothly, but it looks like it's now or never so I jump into my biggest worry at the moment. "Unfortunately, Calista is the one causing the issues at the country club. What's to stop her creating havoc at the Thorny Toad?"

We bump over a buckled portion of the road as we gain the top of the hill. Both sides are lined with old oaks, moss hanging from ancient branches overhead and creating an eerie canopy. But in the car lights cutting through the foggy layer, I can see down into the valley below. The old metal works building seems to be glowing slightly from a few well-placed solar lights in the parking lot.

"Well, you need to get her to cross over," Rosie offers.

"I'm not exactly sure how. She seemed pretty set on keeping Ty for herself, so she doesn't have the desire to leave him."

Mama scoffs. "This is just plain crazy."

I skim through another paragraph in the book. "About as crazy as our family having a stupid curse. I'm not really finding anything in here that can help me understand it."

Mama leans over an inch, eyeing the book. "What exactly are you reading?"

I hold up the thin book to show her the gold embossed title, even though her eyes on are on the road again. "*A Thornhollow History, Volume I.*"

"There's something about the curse in there?"

"So far, no." I slide the book onto the dash, frustrated. "Although, it does mention what Mr. Uphill told me earlier in regard to the fact that Tabitha was run out of Williamsburg for being a witch."

"A witch? Oh, that's ridiculous." Mama scoffs again. "She was an herbalist. A healer. At least that's what my mama told me."

"Many women have been accused of witchcraft for less." Rosie sits forward, squinting at the approaching building. "I'm surprised Uphill shared his precious book with you, Ava."

"Why is that?"

"He's held such a grudge against Miss Willa, I was afraid he'd carry it over onto you."

Mama and I both glance at her. "Grudge about what?" I ask.

Fern snuggles under Rosie's chin, the dog's dark bulbous eyes reflecting the parking lot lights. "Tabby. He claims she was digging in his gardenias all the time. Miss Willa always said she was doing her business in them and that's why they flourished. Mr. Uphill didn't find that funny."

Mama and Rosie both snicker. I don't. "Did he ever threaten the cat?"

"All the time." Rosie waves a hand as if to dismiss it. "He

doesn't have it in in him, though. Uphill wouldn't hurt a fly, much less a cat."

The bar's lighted sign has the first T blanked out, reading *Horny Toad*, instead of *Thorny*. "Classy," I murmur as Mama finds a parking spot under a giant elm tree.

The outside is decorated with fall items, and there are a handful of cars in the lot. Music from a jukebox filters out, but when I step onto the gravel and watch Logan and Brax's vehicles pull in, I'm a little disappointed by the atmosphere.

The building exterior is three shades of gunmetal grey, and in the yellowy illumination from the parking lights, rust and an assortment of graffiti cheerfully accent the steel walls. There's a rickety set of stairs, leading to a freshly painted red door. A vinyl banner reminds patrons they must be eighteen and tells them dogs are welcome, but to leave their guns in their vehicles.

If I was shooting a horror movie, this might be a good backdrop. The biggest wedding in Thornhollow in the past fifty years? Not so much.

"Yup," I mutter as my confidence in the plan plunges. "Ty is gonna have to love Miranda to the very depths of his soul to get her to marry him here."

Chapter Twenty-Six

✤

The interior of the building surprises me, but then it *is* Brax who's revived this place. His decorating skills rival Martha Stewart's.

Rhys is behind the giant 1920s bar that wraps around the center of the vast open main area, creating a focal point. Between two support beams, they've custom built mirrored shelving and decked it out with tiny lights that showcase the numerous bottles of liquor.

To my left is a generous dance floor where couples move to an '80s pop song. To the right are multiple high-back booths with tables, some occupied by patrons enjoying a drink and conversation and a few others reading palms, laying out tarot cards, and giving advice, supposedly inspired by angels, spirit guides, and animals.

Scattered tables and chairs populate the area around the dance floor, and far in the rear, an opaque screen and display of plants and a wishing well hides what I believe to be the kitchen. I can see the tall vent stack reaching up into the open ceiling and out the roof.

As befitting the season, plenty of pumpkins, gourds, apples, and brightly colored leaves lend the place a fall atmosphere. A sandwich board near the door announces a drink special—The Cinnamon Apple, a mix of flavored Schnapps, apple juice with a cinnamon stick garnish.

Someone hails Mama and she excuses herself to go make small talk. Rosie spots her grandmother and ventures to her booth, Fern out of sight in her tote. Queenie's phone rings and she takes the call outside so she can hear over the music.

I remain standing between Logan and Brax, feeling my hopes rising as I imagine transforming the interior to the Snow White wedding of Miranda's dreams.

"What do you think?" Brax asks, a smile of pride on his face.

"It's wonderful," I respond.

Rhys spots us as he sets a beer in front of a patron at the bar. His smile is big and warm as he rushes out to greet us. "Do my eyes deceive me, or is this little Ava Fantome?"

Rhys isn't much taller than I am but acts like an older brother, pulling me into a warm embrace. His fair skin, freckles, and slight frame are in direct contrast to Brax's features, but the unconditional love and friendliness is the same.

"I'm so sorry about Mina," he says. "She was a bright star around here."

"It's good to see you, and about that..." I hesitate a moment. "Why exactly was she working here?"

Rhys leans in conspiratorially. "She talked to ghosts, honey."

I know he's teasing, but I'm still in need of some clarification. "She was offering mediumship readings?"

He pats my hand. "Everybody has to make a living, hon. She could have charged a lot more. We told her all the time that her prices were far too cheap, didn't we, Brax? But she wanted to help folks, and she certainly did us. We wouldn't be here if it hadn't been for her."

My aunt certainly got around in the aid department. "What do you mean? How did she help you?"

He wiggles his fingers. "She worked her voodoo on old man Broussard. He owns this place and she told him his mother wanted him to rent it to us. That Mama Broussard believed in all this stuff and she'd done raised him better than to turn his nose up at a couple of gay guys and some decent people the Lord had blessed with extraordinary gifts. Broussard turned three shades of red, from what I hear, and we signed the rental agreement that afternoon. He even waived the security fee."

Once more my heart pangs at my aunt's sweet soul. This town is indeed going to miss her, and she's left big shoes for anyone to fill.

That thought compounds my feelings of her being loved by so many. Who would ever think of killing her?

Maybe Mama's right. Maybe I'm barking up the wrong tree with the autopsy.

On the heels of that, a cascade of images and sounds fly through my head like an old video tape on rewind…the broken necklace in the creek, the naked woman who turned into a cat, the antique book with a lock in the old trunk.

Could there be something inside that book worth killing for? Am I back to wondering if I actually hear Tabitha and inanimate objects talking to me? The cat had clearly said, "He took it." He, meaning a man, right?

Brax waves a hand in front of my face, "Earth to Ava. You still with us, girl?"

I snap out of it. "Sorry. Just thinking about Aunt Willa."

He motions around at the place. "So, what do you think about the layout? Can you fix this place up for the wedding?"

Rhys's eyes go wide. "You're getting married?" The question is practically shrieked and, even with the jukebox warbling, draws the attention of folks nearby.

I smile, embarrassed. "Oh no. No, no. We need a new spot for the Burnett/Durham wedding, that's all. The country club is no longer an option, and the wedding is in two days."

He throws his head back and chortles. "You want to have it here? Good luck with that, hon. Nancy Durham would rather eat crow than let her precious son get within spitting distance of me."

The song ends and another begins. "Why?" Brax asks.

"Don't you remember? Back in school?" Rhys flips a bar towel from one shoulder to the other, sending a scowl Logan's way. "Ty, Mr. All-Star football player, liked to prank me. Put itching powder in my pants, keyed my car, taunted me in front of his friends all the time. The last straw for me was when he kept bullying my sister to do his chemistry homework. She turned him down and he was dating Calista then, who threatened to beat Jenny up if she didn't help Ty get a passing grade so he didn't get kicked off the team."

"Calista, huh?" I'm older than Rhys, as is Logan, and I don't know about any of this.

"I punched Ty in the mouth, got suspended, too, but it was worth it. I had Jenny carry a digital recorder and tape Calista threatening her. Ty was on there as well, saying he would beat me up if she didn't cooperate. Ty got a two-game suspension is all, but punching him in the nose and seeing the look on his face was priceless."

Logan shifts at my side. "I never heard anything about that."

Rhys gives him a once-over. "You were away at college then, pretty boy, and Nancy Durham kept a lid on it. No way she wanted anyone in this town knowing some skinny gay kid broke her son's nose."

I think of Calista and her temper. No wonder she has the strength, even as a ghost, to create havoc. "You haven't had any weird issues with this place since you opened, have you?"

Both Rhys and Brax give me blank stares.

"You know, electrical or plumbing stuff?"

Rhys shakes his head dismissively. "Not since the grand opening. We had a grease fire in the kitchen and the fridge went out that day, but after your aunt did a clearing on the place to get rid of negative energy hanging around, everything has been great."

I suspect the "negative energy" has a name, and perhaps Calista has caused more than toilets to explode. But if Aunt Willa found a way to keep her out of this place, I'm thrilled. It means it's safe, and we can hold the wedding and reception here, poltergeist-free.

"Pencil us in," I tell Rhys. "And thank you. I have to convince the Durhams this is our only choice, but if I can we'll need the place all day Saturday and Saturday night."

Rhys wiggles his fingers again." You better have some of your aunt's voodoo up your sleeves, hon." He kisses my cheek. "Good luck."

Voodoo and luck... If that's what it takes, I may be in big, big trouble.

Chapter Twenty-Seven

❧❀❧

"**Y**ou know there's another place that might work."

Logan's face is partly in shadow, the dash light falling like lace across his features. We're in his car, heading back to town.

He's taking me home since Brax and Queenie have to start making plans for the possible wedding, and Rosie's son, little Mike, was scared of a skeleton in his closet. His dad couldn't see it, and little Mike insisted he couldn't go to bed until Rosie came home and got rid of it. Mama volunteered to drive her since I had wanted to hang around long enough to make sure Calista didn't appear and discuss a few of the details with Queenie about the food.

If Calista is haunting Ty and Miranda, the true test will come when I inform them of the Thorny Toad's potential.

Logan insisted to my mother he would drop me safely at Aunt Willa's doorstep, and it made sense with him living across the street.

Still, I feel uncomfortable sitting in the car, driving a deserted county road, and caught between thoughts of ghosts and disastrous weddings, along with unbidden fantasies about him.

Absentmindedly, I rub the spot on the back of my head. The lump is nearly gone, only a bit of soreness left. Did Logan really save my life? "Another place?" I echo. At least, I can explain Tabby's reaction earlier today—she hates Mr. Uphill, not Logan. "I'm all ears. Spill."

A smile crosses his face and he glances sideways at me. "Have you considered the vineyard?"

"The winery? Your family's, you mean?"

He nods.

At that moment, we pass a roadside sign advertising Cross Family Winery as if on cue. A beautiful setting, plenty of space, plenty of alcohol...my head is suddenly full of ideas.

There's just one problem—or three. "There's no building for it, no kitchen. And your mother would never allow it with the tour on Sunday."

We pass the Welcome to Thornhollow sign and Logan heads north, ignoring the turn to take us home. "Let me show you what I'm thinking."

The road heading north toward the mountains in the distance is the complete opposite of the one we've been on. Well paved, lighted, and sprinkled with more signs directing folks to the winery.

The ads proclaim the Cross Wines' awards, showing giant glasses of both reds and whites, and even displaying smiling families, as if the fifty acres of property is a vacation destination.

We pass a sign that offers an invitation: "Bring the whole family for a day of play."

Logan offhandedly points at the signage, the headlights slipping over the boy and girl in the picture. "We added a play area and a pumpkin patch, and we even have a corn maze."

So while mom and dad get tanked on samples, the kids can play. "That's nice. Why?"

As if he's reading my mind, he gives me another grin, this one sardonic. "It's good for business, but honestly I think it's a jab from Mom to me."

"A jab about what?"

"The fact I haven't settled down and started a family." He slows, turning on the winding road heading for the estate. "Does your mother harass you about that kind of stuff?"

Come to think of it, no, but now I know the reason. She's afraid I might end up a widow. "Mama's so busy being mayor she doesn't ride me about much, although she does want me to move home."

He pulls into the long, oak-lined drive. "She misses you."

The Cross acreage stretches out before us, and we climb one of the hills covered with grapevines. "I miss her too, but..."

"You have a career, a life, in Atlanta," he finishes for me.

There's a lot of teasing in his voice and my hackles rise. We wind around several corners and two large buildings appear. In the dark, I can make out rows of vines in the distance, a couple of sheds, and an assortment of trucks and other vehicles. "I do," I confirm. "I'm only a few hours away and I come home when I can."

He passes near one of the large outbuildings, this one made of logs, and we get out. It's dark out here, far from the house, and the stars twinkle overhead like a blanket of lights. "Seems like we could use your talents and gumption here."

"Gumption? Did you actually just say that?"

He laughs.

I hesitate, wanting to disagree with his analysis, but sensing this is a trap. "Even if I were to move here, I can't fill Aunt Willa's shoes. No one can."

Logan stands for a moment gazing up at the stars, and I

follow suit. They are breathtaking. "Gives you perspective, doesn't it?" he asks.

I sense this is part of the trap to make me feel wanted here in Thornhollow and give up my city life. But, he's right. As I stare at the stars and think about everything that's happened this week, I feel a lot calmer.

Picking our way across gravel and various flower beds, he leads me to the south end of the building. Double barn doors open to a vast, dark interior. "You could bring your own shoes to fill."

He disappears inside as I sputter. A series of overhead lights come on high in the rafters. The logs are visible inside, too, and the scent of cool air and cedar meets my nose.

There are dozens of round wooden tables and chairs upended on top of them. There's a very large, very elaborate bar made solely out of wood. There's a giant open dance floor, raised slightly off the ground, and I see double barn doors at that end.

Logan opens his arms and motions at the rustic interior. "We have a bar, men's and women's restrooms, and plenty of seating. You can get more seating by opening up those back doors and setting up tented areas outside. We can bring up the picnic tables from the family area or borrow chairs from the church."

The ideas about holding the wedding and reception here come rushing back and I turn in a circle, allowing my imagination to take it all in. The rustic nature of the place is actually perfect for a fall wedding with the forest theme that Miranda has picked.

"This is amazing." I visualize where to put the DJ and how to wrap the pillars and open beams with lights. "You've been holding out on me."

He chuckles. "Not intentionally. We never use this place, and I kind of forgot about it. I haven't been in here in years."

Dust and cobwebs confirm that no one has been inside in a

long time. Still, it's in great shape. "I didn't realize you even had this place." I've never been in this section of the winery, and the one time I visited years ago was when mother held a dinner in the main hall for her backers.

"My great-grandad bought the land and he and my grandma turned it into the winery in the early days of the1900s. Then came Prohibition, and the place became a speakeasy."

The history of this building intrigues me. Relaxing my sight, a grey fog seems to seep from the wood and I can imagine—or maybe see—the ghosts of the past laughing and dancing and having a great time. It's like watching a black and white film superimposed over the current scene. I hear music, and the air is thick with cigarette smoke and perfume.

A good-looking guy in a suit catches my eye and winks. Yep, definitely ghosts. But they seem pretty benign. Like lost in time, but in no hurry to move on.

"There's no kitchen." Logan's voice jars me back to the present. "We'll need to figure out a way to—"

"Logan?" Mrs. Cross appears in the open doorway, hugging a silk robe tight around her neck. Her eyes flick over me, and she looks embarrassed. It could be the yellow curlers adorning the sides and top of her head. "What in heaven's name are you two doing out here at this time of night?"

Chapter Twenty-Eight

A s Logan tells his mother about using the former speakeasy for the wedding and reception, her brows go up and her mouth turns down. "You can't be serious," she says.

I step up to Logan's defense, warming to the idea even more. "It's the ideal venue. The space, the beautiful setting..." The fact it has dry floors and working toilets is a bonus, too. "Think of how much wine you'll sell, and the potential for future events that could boost your business."

I see a spark of interest and realize appealing to the businesswoman in her is a good idea, but the argument I knew was coming surfaces. "We have the tour on Sunday." Her perfectly arched eyebrows are knitted so tight they're nearly a single brow. "I can't possibly host a reception on Saturday night."

"Actually, it seems like the perfect combination, if you ask me." I try to paint a picture for her as vividly as possible, pointing at the different areas of the space. "This area could host even more tourists for the tasting ceremony on Sunday. It will already be decorated and we can add a splash of fall, and even Christmas, to everything. It's never too early to get people thinking about gift-giving for the holidays. Imagine a selection of gift baskets—maybe do some with the Durham candies in them.

My excitement is growing and I see her brows relaxing and my vision dawning in her eyes. "This could be a whole new partnership for you. I mean, wine and chocolates? Win-win."

Why she hasn't thought of this before is beyond me, and from her expression she seems to be thinking a similar thing.

But then she clues me in. "The Durham family is very particular about who they do business with. We tried a special promotion many years ago and it didn't work out. They won't go for it, and, frankly, I can't offer up this space to them. I'm sorry."

"But, Mom." Logan gives me an apologetic look as his mother turns and walks away. He charges after her, and after a second I hustle out on his heels. Heart sinking, but determined, I'm not letting this opportunity pass me by.

With all the relationships in Thornhollow, some going back generations, there's more to this story and the past between the Cross and Durham families than she's letting on, I'd bet my morning coffee on it. I don't necessarily need to know what it is, but it's time it ended. Both families have been in this town for decades, running successful businesses and trying to outdo each other. If only they would work together.

"Mom, wait." Logan gently grabs her arm and stops her. "Hear us out. Ty and Miranda have nowhere else to go. Ava's right, this could be a golden opportunity for us."

"Our only other option is the Thorny Toad," I add.

Helen Cross screws up her face. "Oh, lord."

"Yes, exactly." I try not to take offense out of deference to Brax and Rhys, and also try to play up the idea that one of the town's foremost families may be reduced to having a wedding south of town. "While this setting"—I wave my hand at the night sky and the winsome sloping valley in the distance—"is a fairy-tale. Perfect for the Snow White wedding that Miranda's dreamed about since she was a girl. I promise you won't have any extra work—I'll handle everything—and I'll secure a deal with the Durhams for a wine and chocolate partnership, if only for this weekend. I wholeheartedly believe they'll see the potential is truly unlimited. Imagine events taking place here for New Year's, Valentine's Day, summer weddings, the holidays... framing the winery as an event and wedding destination could double or triple your profit margins."

Logan nods his agreement. "At least try this one event," he prompts. "Like Ava said, we'll handle the details. You won't have to lift a finger."

"And," I offer, lowering my voice to a confidential tone, "if we pull this off for Ty and Miranda, the Durhams and the Burnetts will be in your debt for generations to come."

Her curlered head tilts as she studies me. There's a long pause as my words sink in. "I have your word this won't interfere with the tour on Sunday?"

As long as Calista doesn't make an appearance. I smile big and send a silent wish up to the stars overhead. "I promise."

Chapter Twenty-Nine

There's a man sitting on the front steps when Logan drops me at the house.

"You've got company." Logan eases to the curb and I squint at the figure waiting for me. "I'll walk you up."

There's a note of protectiveness in his voice. I didn't leave the porch lights on, but their honey glow shines out anyway. I wonder who might have turned them on—is Aunt Willa inside waiting for me? Did Tabby turn into a woman again? At this stage, nothing would surprise me.

My visitor is backlit, his face in shadows. "You don't have to." Yet, I stay planted in my seat. "It's not really necessary. Is it?"

He shrugs. "Ty's probably here because he's worried about Miranda, but if he's upset I can convince him we have things covered."

Ah, Ty Durham, I'm not sure I would have recognized him even if he were standing directly under the light. "Are you two friends?"

"Nope." He puts the car in park and kills the lights. "But we're both members of the athletic boosters. We're...acquaintances."

There's a part of me that wants to extract retribution from this guy for terrorizing Rhys. But that was so many years ago, and, hopefully, he grew out of that bully stage. Still, Logan's protectiveness keeps the warning bells in my head ringing. "Do you know anything about the night Calista died?"

The street light down past Mr. Uphill's place gives the sidewalk a soft ambience and reflects in Logan's eyes when he turns to me. "She and Ty were out partying, he was drunk, she took the wheel. I doubt she was more sober than he was, and unfortunately the accident happened. He always blamed himself because he survived."

I nod, studying Ty as he leans forward and puts his elbows on his knees, watching us back.

"Two former football players, both from prestigious Thornhollow families, and you're only acquaintances?"

He ignores the question and asks one of his own—one that completely takes me off guard. "Want to go to the football game tomorrow night?"

"What?"

"Think you'll have time? It doesn't start until seven and we can leave early if you need to get back here to work on stuff."

Homecoming. Of course, the whole town will be at the game, cheering on the team.

I'm baffled he would ask me, and I stammer for an answer. I'm not a football fan and I can't imagine taking a few hours off to watch the game. Nor do I want to. "It's sweet of you to ask…"

He doesn't let me finish, reaching for his door handle "Great. We'll grab dinner in between the parade and the game."

Did he just ask me out on a…a *date*?

Before I can beg off, he bails from the car. Head spinning, I climb out as well.

"I think you misunderstood," I tell him when we hit the sidewalk.

Ty stands, hands sliding into his pockets. "Logan, Ava." He

nods at each of us as Logan opens the gate and ushers me through.

I guess this isn't the best time to correct Logan's assumption, the event planner in me stepping forward. "Hi, Ty." I offer my hand as I stride confidently up to him. "I'm glad you're here. Would you like to come in? Have some tea?"

His hair is a dishwater shade of blond, even in the warm glow of the porch light. Tight lines accentuate his mouth and full lips. "No ma'am, it's late, I know, but I heard you were still out and about, scouting places for my wedding."

Nothing goes unnoticed in this town, apparently even my whereabouts. "We have two very strong candidates," I tell him with a smile. "Either will work well, and I'd be happy to go over the details with you and Miranda tonight if you'd like. Your parents are welcome, too."

I assume the elder Burnetts and Durhams are paying for everything, so it's imperative I get their buy-in.

He kicks at a small rock on the sidewalk, head lowered. "You sure it's even worth trying at this point?" His voice is quiet, his down-home, boy-next-door look sincere as he raises his gaze to mine.

Once more, I'm caught off guard. "Of course, it is! There's no reason to postpone the wedding because of the country club flooding. Which I explained to Miranda earlier today. Your dream wedding is still viable."

He glances over at Mr. Uphill's. "I mean, the whole thing. It just feels like..."

At his hesitation, Logan moves closer. "Like what?"

Ty's gaze seems a million miles away. The cool night air turns frosty. "Like God, or the universe, or whatever, doesn't want me to get married."

"Look out," a croaky voice says.

Great. The door knocker.

"Here she comes," one of the gargoyles adds.

A gust of wind flips hair into my face. Neither of the men hears the voices, but I glance around, tensing in expectation. If only Ty knew the truth. I look for signs that Calista is with us, listen for her voice. "You and Miranda are meant to be together, I'm sure of it."

"No they're not!" The ghost shouts right in my ear, making me jump and bump hard into Logan.

He straightens me up, keeping a firm hand on my arm. "Hey, are you okay?"

I'm grateful for the warmth of his hand and his strength. "Just tired. It's been a long day—a long couple of days, in fact."

Ty visibly shudders, as if cold. "You know, when your aunt was here, I thought we might actually pull this off. But now, I'm not feeling it."

"Pull this off?" The phrase strikes me as odd. Does Ty know he's being haunted by his ex? Did Aunt Willa tell him? "Is there anything you want me to know, anything odd that's been happening to you or Miranda? What we might call bad luck? Do you feel like you're...cursed?"

He pales visibly under the porch light, nearly looking like a ghost himself. "How did you...?"

That's why Miranda's had such a strong reaction to my claim that Prissy Barnes is jinxed. "I have a bit of my aunt's gift." I hope that if Aunt Willa told him about Calista, he'll get my drift. I really *am* tired and it seems as if the only way to "pull this off" is to convince Ty I can take over where Aunt Willa left off— ghost or not.

I only have to figure out how she planned to stop Calista from ruining the wedding. "I can help you and Miranda. I just need a little time."

Logan looks at me sharply. "Your aunt's gift? You can see...ghosts?"

My stomach falls. He knows?

Well, the cat's out of the bag.

I bet he's rethinking that date.

Before I can answer him, the rocking chair on the porch starts to move back and forth and a woman materializes. She looks eerily like Belatrix LeStrange from the Harry Potter movies.

The thing is, she also resembles my friend Winter on a bad hair day.

I step closer to the porch, eyeing her and wondering if Winter has somehow teleported herself to my aunt's house. "Winter?"

The men look at the chair, back at me. The woman smiles. "She said not to scare you—that I should appear *normal*." She makes air quotes around the word and rolls her eyes. "No imitating Endora from *Bewitched* or the gal from *I Dream of Jeannie*."

My heart sinks. It's not Winter, but it *is* her new spirit guide —a snarky, angel-like being who has a thing for '70s sitcoms. "Persephone?"

"Who's Winter?" Logan scans the porch and front yard. "Who's Persephone?"

He and Ty can't see her any more than they can see Calista. I'm not sure how I can, but her timing is the worst. "No one," I tell him and then to Ty, I plead, "Don't worry. I can handle this. Round up everyone you want and bring them here at nine tomorrow morning, okay? We'll get things sorted out and everything will be fine."

Persephone snickers, and as she rocks back and forth, Calista's voice rings out. "I will never let Ty go!"

"Looks like you've got yourself a wild one there," Persephone intones, and her gaze goes to a spot behind Ty's shoulders.

"You can see her?" I ask automatically, forgetting Logan and Ty are both still here. They look at me with a mix of concern and confusion, but I can tell Logan's assuming I'm talking to ghosts.

Persephone chuckles. "Can't you?"

I shake my head and notice how Ty is hunching his shoulders. He shudders again. "I'll think about it." He brushes by Logan, heading down the sidewalk. "Sorry about your aunt."

He walks away, disappearing into the shadows. Only the *tap, tap, tap* of his shoes echoes through the soft night stillness until that's gone, too.

"Are there ghosts here?" Logan asks quietly.

I give him a look, words deserting me. How much does he really know? How much does he *want* to know?

He seems to accept the silence as an affirmative. He takes my arm again. "Let's get you inside. You're right, it's been a long day."

Yep, he's definitely going to rescind his offer for the date. I just hope he keeps his word to help me set up the old speakeasy for the reception.

We start up the steps. "Yes, it has. Thank you," I tell him. "Like I said, it's been a stressful week." I rub the back of my head, hoping to play up the possibility my odd behavior could be due to the concussion. "I'm so grateful for all of your help today. I mean it. You may have single-handedly saved this wedding."

At the praise, I see the flash of that familiar grin. "You don't have to butter me up, Ava."

We stand in front of the door and he moves closer, rubbing my arm. His eyes catch the light and glow as he looks down at me. "You've been through a lot and you're trying to help everyone out with this when you don't really have to. I'm here for you, okay?"

Persephone snickers again, but I ignore her. I'm mesmerized by Logan's eyes, a midnight blue under the light, and feeling pretty damn confident that I *will*, come heck or high water, get all of this figured out and save the day.

Winter has sent Persephone, and I have my aunt's book

upstairs that must hold some tips and tricks to handle Calista. I'll figure out a way to free Ty and Miranda from this poltergeist, get them married, and let them live their happily ever after.

Then, I'll cross Tim Shackleford over, figure out if my aunt was murdered and, if so, who did it.

"It's been a joint effort," I tell Logan and kick myself for sounding so lame. "You, Rosie, Brax, Queenie... You're the true heroes."

His lips come down on mine—soft, warm, and comforting. It stirs something deep inside of me, and white-hot heat shoots straight to my toes. "Humble like Willa Rae, too," he says in a hushed tone.

I sigh, kissing him back. Relishing the feel of him, my head spins in a happy way and my legs turn to jelly.

Chapter Thirty

Logan breaks the kiss after a bit, leaving me lightheaded. "We've got a big day tomorrow. Get some rest."

He leaves his car parked at the curb, closing the gate behind him and jogging across the street to his place.

"That's some nice eye candy," Persephone snarks, startling me.

"Forgot you were here," I mutter, and then reluctantly face her. "Any chance you know how to chase off a poltergeist?"

"I fought the big, bad Master last December with Winter. I think I can handle a pesky spirit."

"Technically, Winter and her sisters fought that demon, but"—I unlock and open the door—"I suppose you did help a little."

"I am completely unappreciated."

All three cats circle my feet, crying and whining. Persephone simply appears in the front room, rather than using the open door to enter. The cat knocker says, "She's trouble." The gargoyles agree, and I slam the door shut on them.

Interestingly enough, Persephone doesn't seem to pick up on

the fact that inanimate objects are talking. I'm not sure if that's reassuring or not.

Lights magically come on as she half-walks, half-floats over to Rosie's desk. Her hair and clothes morph from dark to light, the change in appearance now roughly resembling a Dolly Parton imitation—big hair, long nails, and an hourglass figure. "Winter said you're seeing and hearing spirits more than you used to." Even her voice is lighter, with a honeyed Southern accent.

I hang up my coat. Chilled, I rub my arms, wishing I could think about the kiss and Logan rather than rehashing what's happened since my aunt died.

Turning up the heat on the furnace dial, I recite the bare facts. Then I head to the kitchen to feed the cats. "Possibly the knock on the head did it. I'm hoping it fades like my lump is doing."

"Doubtful. It's the trip you took across the veil that ramped up your abilities. You're a spirit walker now, not just a medium."

I lean against the kitchen door, feeling drained. "A what? You mean like Winter?"

She touches a few of the tea cups and saucers my aunt collected, displayed on an intricate wooden shelf Uncle Saddler made for her. "You're a spirit walker. Winter's a shaman. You died and came back. You've seen the other side. *My* side."

"Lucky me," I murmur sarcastically.

She smiles. "Pretty cool there, huh?"

"Honestly, I don't remember anything about it. I mean, I know Logan said I stopped breathing and he had to resuscitate me, but maybe he was wrong, or maybe it happened so fast I didn't even know it."

"Time runs differently when crossing the veil. Space, too. What may have seemed instantaneous to you may have been hours or days in this dimension." She fiddles with a sequin on her elaborate pantsuit. "Logan? Is that the guy who kissed you?"

"Yeah, him. If he hadn't found me, I might not be here."

The cats, having finished their meals, wander over to me. All three watch Persephone from a distance. Arthur and Lancelot stay close to my ankles, while Tabitha flicks her marmalade tail at Persephone before exiting the kitchen and disappearing up the stairs.

"Better keep a close eye on that one." The angel cocks her head at the spot where Tabby walked out. "There's some bad juju around her."

I'm not sure of Persephone's definition of *bad juju* but I get the general drift and take offense. "I think she's my ancestor, Tabitha Holloway. She's some kind of shapeshifter, I guess. She was one of the original founders of our town."

"Never trust shapeshifters, and that one has some B.I.G. secrets,"

I think about Winter's boyfriend, Ronan. Her sister Spring's boyfriend, too. They're both shapeshifters. In fact, the sisters' handyman and his mother are as well. I like them all and find them to be more trustworthy and honorable than many "normal" human beings. "I happen to like shapeshifters, although I'm still having trouble wrapping my mind around the idea."

Persephone crosses her arms over her buxom chest and gives me a look that suggests I'm being stubborn. Reminds me of Mama.

"Forget the shapeshifting," I tell her. "How do you know there's bad juju around Tabby?"

She eyes me with a bit of peevishness. "Because I'm a spirit guide...?"

Her tone implies I'm a dunce.

Maybe I am. "Well, Miss High and Mighty, if you know so much, then have a seat and fill me in. We can start with who murdered my aunt? What does it have to do with my family's curse? And is my dad exempt from the curse as long as he stays away from this town? Also, I really need to know how to get rid of this *gift*, and"—I nearly ask what should I do about Logan —"how to get rid of Calista."

A laugh issues from her mouth, her peevishness gone. "I couldn't give you those answers even if I knew them—which I don't, for the most part. I'm still a peon in the spirit guide realm. Still have my training wheels on, so to speak. I *can* offer suggestions, and pass on hints from the Big Guy." She points heavenward. "But those are few and far between, thanks to you having free will and the fact you have to learn life lessons. You know, all that jazz."

She pushes off from the desk and begins to wander. I follow her, trying to think of an argument or a persuasion. She takes in Uncle Saddler's bookshelves, running her hands along the spines, then examines an antique clock on the fireplace mantel. With a sigh and flourish, she turns back to me. "So let's start with the most pressing item on your list and see what I can help with, shall we?"

"Everything on my list is pressing. I'm not sure how to pick only one."

"Then it's the perfect time to meditate."

My mouth falls open. I'd forgotten just how challenging— and bonkers—this spirit guide is. I barely met her when I visited Winter and her sisters to help with the demon last winter, and thank goodness for that. "I don't have time to meditate, Persephone. Get real."

"The first lesson of spirit walking and controlling the veil is stilling the mind. You need to practice handling ghosts, and you can't do that until you know how to control your gift."

"Oh *puuleaze*," I whine. "Just tell me how to get rid of Calista."

Ignoring me, she wiggles her fingers and sends two pillows from the couch to the floor. Plunking down on one of them and arranging herself in a cross-legged position, she assumes a meditation posture with eyes closed and thumbs and forefingers touching as her hands rest on her knees. "If you want my help, we do things my way."

Arthur and Lancelot glide over to her, cautiously, sniffing the air and her clothes. Lancelot's big green eyes turn to me and then he sits, not right next to her but close.

Arthur circles her several times, a bit more standoffish, before he jumps on the sofa and lies down behind her. He also looks at me and blinks, his tail flicking back and forth.

Psychic abilities or not, I know my cats. Lancelot believes I should try the meditation and Arthur's letting me know he'll protect me if necessary.

Frustrated, I stomp off. Then find myself circling back.

With a dramatic sigh Mama would be proud of I plop onto the empty cushion and close my eyes.

Chapter Thirty-One

I fall asleep and dream of Aunt Willa. We are sitting in her kitchen, both of us much younger. She makes my favorite mint tea, putting honey in it.

She sets the cup in front of me and sits. "You need to go up in the attic."

"I don't like the attic," my little girl self replies.

From the floral sugar bowl she scoops out a spoonful of pink crystals and I watch them dissolve in the warm liquid. "Nothing can harm you."

A blue butterfly lands on the sugar bowl. In order not to answer—or argue—I sip the tea. There's a slight bitterness under the mint flavor.

The dream shifts and I'm now at the open door of the staircase leading up to the attic. The darkness above looms over me, blanketing the upper steps.

"I don't like the attic," I whisper. My legs and feet are frozen to the wood planks of the floor. The butterfly beats its wings around my head.

"Find Teddy." My aunt points a hand toward the shadows overhead. "He's waiting for you. He'll be so happy to see you."

Teddy, the stuffed bear I carried everywhere and slept with until I was too old for it, seems to beckon me. A part of me wonders why I abandoned him to the scary darkness above.

The butterfly wings its way up several steps, returns to my face, flies back to the steps. Back and forth it goes, as if it too believes I should journey into the shadows.

"There's nothing to fear," Aunt Willa says. "You're always protected inside this house. You must learn to control your abilities, control how far you step into the veil and the doorway between worlds." With final emphasis she says, "Find the bear."

Do butterflies ever feel scared? The blue wings flutter about my face, the tiniest of breezes tickling my skin as it urges me to follow. It glides up the stairwell in lazy arcs and a chill sweeps over me, raising goosebumps on the flesh of my arms.

Placing one foot on the bottom tread, I see Aunt Willa smile. As my weight shifts, the moment I fully commit, a bright, blinding light fills the stairwell. A burst of cold air blasts me back.

I jerk awake, gasping, and find myself outside sitting on the cold damp lawn.

Stars twinkle overhead and the goose flesh is real on my bare arms.

"Get up." Persephone appears in front of me. "Get in the house, now!"

"Why?" Wooziness weights my head and makes my ears buzz from the dramatic shift of the dream world into the real one. "What am I doing out here?"

"Sleepwalking," she hisses. "In case you weren't aware, you stink at meditating."

"Why are you talking so softly?"

She hitches a thumb over her shoulder toward the tree line along the fence. I hear movement there, and, gaining my feet, I brush damp leaves from my backside. I lower my voice now, too. "I had a dream."

"I know." She glances toward Mr. Uphill's. "We'll discuss it inside."

A breeze rustles the leaves and lifts strands of my hair. I hear a puff of laughter in the air and a new wave of arctic air snakes down my spine.

Calista is back.

"Ava?" A man's voice calls softly across the lawn. Mr. Uphill appears at the hedgerow, the very top of his head and eyes barely visible. He must be standing on tiptoes. "Everything okay?"

I lift a hand in greeting and fumble for an excuse to be out here this time of night. "Yes, fine. Tabby got out."

Although I can only see the top of his head and eyes, I know he's screwing up his nose. "At 4 a.m.?"

It's four o'clock in the morning? I must have slept longer than I realized. I wonder what *he's* doing out here this early. Probably working on his precious flower bushes again. "You know cats," I offer weakly.

"I saw Ty Durham hanging around rather late last night. How's it going with the wedding?"

"Fine."

His eyebrows quirk, "I heard the Burnetts are calling it off."

Another blast of icy air hits me in the back of the neck. Calista's voice rings in my ears as she screams at me, reciting the same litany of guarantees that Ty is hers and she'll never let him go.

In my mind's eye, I see the butterfly bravely going up the stairs. I remember Aunt Willa's words about my abilities and the veil. I'm sick of this ghost and her capacity to have so much control over the situation.

A spurt of anger flashes through me and I feel myself mentally shoving the ghost away. I visualize her landing on her butt.

At the same moment, I hear her suck in a breath. Her voice

grows distant as she curses at me. Persephone, apparently still able to see her, watches something a few yards away and quirks one corner of her mouth in a grin.

The sensation of pushing Calista empowers me. I nod at Mr. Uphill and start for the house. The back door to the porch is wide open and I hope I won't actually need to search for Tabby come sunrise. "We have a few details to work out, but the wedding and reception are still on. See you at the parade."

Calista attempts to chase me as I draw close to the porch, but once more I send a mental shove her way. With an angry *hurrumph* her frigid energy disappears completely.

Inside, I'm shaking, so I search for my robe and rub my hands together to warm them. I'd love a cup of hot tea, but I'm too impatient to make one. Persephone follows me up the stairs to the second floor. "Where are you going?"

"In the dream, I opened the door at the end of the hall and looked up into the shadows of the attic." I head for it now, flinching when the old door makes a high-pitched squeak. "You were the butterfly, weren't you? You know where I'm going."

She hovers beside me, the darkness above us seeming to ripple a little. "To the attic?"

"Yes." I quell the childhood fear in my stomach. "We're going to the attic."

Chapter Thirty-Two

✿

A click of the single overhead lightbulb brings the attic into view, throwing a deathly pallor on assorted furniture, covered with dusty sheets, old suitcases and trunks, long forgotten rugs, paintings and other miscellanea.

A desk near the back catches my attention. Teddy sits on a stack of books, his brown glass eyes seeming to follow me as I weave around various obstacles to get to him.

Tabby suddenly appears at my feet, nearly tripping me. She meows at me, jumping onto the desk and knocking the bear off. She paws at the top book, and as I bend down to retrieve the stuffed bear I notice how cracked and dusty the leather-bound volume is.

Teddy's not in much better shape, spots of his fur worn, one ear torn, and a side seam unraveling. He smells of dust and dry air. Using one hand, I brush dust away before reverently laying him aside and picking up the book.

The leather creaks as I open the front cover, the inside paper is dry like parchment and stained the color of weak tea. Old-fashioned handwriting with scrolls and flourishes declares this is the diary of Tabitha Holloway.

"This is yours?" I ask the cat.

Even in the dull light, her eyes gleam. Her paws knead at the desktop and I hear her purr. I've never heard her purr and the sound relaxes me slightly.

Persephone has disappeared, and there's no butterfly either. A nearby rocking chair, with a needlepoint pillow, beckons me to have a seat. The light is poor, but I sit and begin devouring the diary.

Virginia, 1788. I have found the true soul mate I have been searching for...

Tabby hops onto my lap as I read. The combination of penmanship, the age of the book itself, and great-great-however-many-times-grandmother's descriptions catapult me back to a different time and place. I read ravenously, barely able to decipher some of the information because of the outdated wording and phrasing, but the gist is there.

Her entries speak of love, companionship, healing and magick. Of dreams and desires. Birth, death, endings, and trans-formation.

By the time I finish, the first rays of sun are peaking over the horizon. Samuel Thornton and Tabitha Holloway were run out of town by his wife Redemption. That one little fact changes much of what I understood from Mr. Uphill's history.

In his rendition, Tabitha seduced Samuel away from his wife and kids, but now I know there's another side to this story, and this one definitely shows a different perspective. It's a fasci-nating account, and as I flip to the last few pages at the back I absentmindedly stroke Tabby's fur. She rubs her head into my hand and the purring continues.

"I'm so sorry this happened to you," I tell her, and she dips her head as if in acknowledgement.

The pages at the back display a family tree—not in the vintage handwriting of Tabby, but my aunt's. Several of the later entries surprise me, and I close the book and sit for a long minute, digesting the information and realizing what it all means.

A floorboard squeaks, startling me out of my thoughts, and Persephone appears. "I believe your poltergeist is a type of revenant."

"What is that?"

"She's tied to someone still alive, and I don't mean like in the sense of you and your aunt. Someone is controlling Calista, and they've purposely brought her back from the grave and sicced her on the happy couple. She'd be a strong poltergeist, but as a revenant? Superpowers."

I sit and rock, my mind volunteering an ugly thought. "Powers strong enough to kill someone?"

Judging by the flicker behind her eyes, Persephone knows what I'm asking and nods her head. "A revenant has been raised by a master. Find the master and you can sever the connection."

"Master?" I shudder at the thoughts of the one called Master in the Whitethorne woods.

"This is different. That was an evil non-living being. The person controlling Calista is human."

I immediately think of Ty but can't imagine the man I met earlier being able to raise a ghost. He obviously has some level of belief in them and considered it bad luck. I can't see him raising Calista and controlling her in order to get out of marrying Miranda. "Could someone raise the ghost without knowing it? Like an accident?"

Again, the spirit guide's eyes let me know she understands. She shakes her big hair. "This raising was deliberate, but it doesn't necessarily mean the person knows how to control the ghost."

"So Calista has a lot of power, the master may not be able to control her."

A nod.

"How do I stop her?"

"Sever the link between them."

I sigh and push out of the chair. "Which I have no idea how to do."

Persephone winks. "You've got me. What else do you need?"

Chapter Thirty-Three

❦

As I get ready to leave the attic, I take one more look at Teddy and replace the diary on the stack of books. Propping him on top, I ask him to keep it safe, and tell him I'll be back. If I'm staying, this attic is going to get a good clean-up. Who knows what other family secrets I might discover?

Movement outside the window on my left draws my attention. I'm looking down into a section of Mr. Uphill's backyard. I move closer to the window, the backyard cast in shades of purple from the coming sunrise. Mr. Uphill and Prissy Barnes are in amongst the gardenias.

As I squint and watch them in the shadows, it appears they're arguing. I observe for several moments, Tabitha jumping on the desk and also peering over the window ledge, and a plan formulates in my mind.

That gardenia patch. The night Mr. Uphill was digging in it...last night catching me sleepwalking. There's something not right about any of it. I feel the thread, the tug, of a mystery pulling at me.

"Come on, grandma."

The cat gives a haughty sniff, as if not appreciating the title. However, she comes with me, Persephone floating behind us.

The back screen door squeaks too much for us to sneak up on the pair, so I lead them out the front, planning a silent trek around the side of the house to the backyard. As I quietly close the wooden door behind us, the cat knocker whispers, "Be careful."

"Thanks for the advice," I whisper back.

Yes, I give up. I'm talking to inanimate objects with no worries about my mental health.

As we tiptoe down the wooden steps, the gargoyle guardians on each side of the railings chatter away at me.

"Yeah, yeah, I hear you," I whisper and keep going.

The three of us sneak around the opposite side of the house, through the lawn, and keep low as we tiptoe over to the hedgerow.

"Why is the wedding still on?" Prissy's voice is rigid even though she's trying to keep the volume down. "You were supposed to make sure Miranda turned to *me*. Why is Ava still here?"

I can't hear Mr. Uphill's reply, possibly because all he does is make a face. Prissy speaks again. "She's the last one of them. We have to get rid of her, then there's no one left of the Holloway line, except the mayor, and she's too old to have more kids."

The blood in my veins turns frosty. I'm the last one of Tabby's descendants, except for Mama, and they want to get rid of us?

Mr. Uphill speaks in a quiet tone, but more calmly. "We don't want to draw attention. I'll make sure the wedding doesn't proceed, and your business will be successful once we run off Ava. We're not doing anything to her, outside of getting her out of town."

Mr. Uphill is working with Prissy to try and sink The Wedding Chapel business? Maybe I misunderstood what she meant about getting rid of us. She's just like her name, prissy, and trying to expand her own business at the expense of my aunt's.

"If you don't get Ty and Miranda to come to me for their event tomorrow," she hisses, "I swear I *will* take matters into my own hands to get rid of Ava."

Another chill runs through me at her words. Just exactly how does she intend to get rid of me? My mind swims back to Aunt Willa's death.

Mr. Uphill says. "Oh, right, because doing that worked so well last time, didn't it?"

Prissy snickers. "Willa had a heart attack and fell in the creek. I have no idea what you are talking about."

Mr. Uphill's tone sharpens. "I warned you not to mess with that stuff. You've created something you can't control."

"You let me worry about Cali."

Cali? Does she mean Calista?"

Persephone is motioning at them and nodding her head, as if reminding me what she said about a revenant. Is it possible Priscilla Barnes purposely raised a ghost to do her bidding? Is that what Mr. Uphill means about her messing with *that stuff?*

Priscilla, who's as down to earth as they come...does she even believe in ghosts?

The sound of the bushes shifting alerts me to Prissy walking away. I stiffen as I hear her stop, sniff. "Do you smell that?" she calls back to Uphill in a stage-whisper.

"What?"

"Over here. It smells like...onion rings."

She's directly on the other side of the hedge. My stomach drops as I realize she smells...me. I flare my nose, my nostrils picking up the faint scent of fried food from the Thorny Toad.

"Who's there?" she demands through the hedge, but I'm sure she can guess.

With a shuffle, the hedge trembles and a hand jets through

the foliage, barely missing my shoulder. I dodge, holding my breath, and freeze once more.

Tabby comes out of nowhere, dashing into the boxwoods and startling Priscilla. She shrieks and her hand disappears.

Mr. Uphill shushes her, swearing under his breath. He's afraid she'll wake his guests. As he apparently chases after Tabby, calling her a litany of names, Priscilla grunts and stomps off.

Shaking, I silently thank the cat and sneak back to the house.

Chapter Thirty-Four

S hivering and shaking, I climb into bed with the cats, my mind numb. Eventually, I fall into a deep sleep, and when I wake, for a brief second I wonder if I dreamt the previous night's shenanigans, including Persephone, but the stains on the cuffs of my pajama bottoms tell me differently.

Once I'm showered and ready for the day, I head downstairs, snag coffee from the pot Rosie has already started, and compartmentalize.

Focus on what you need to do first.

Rosie greets me with a "good morning" and informs me she's already fed the cats. Author, Lancelot, and Tabby are in their usual places in the sunlight coming through the front windows. I swear Tabby winks at me when I walk by.

I wink back, sipping coffee, and tell Rosie about my plan for using the vineyard. "It's an idyllic spot for a wedding, plus I know the Durhams and Crosses could capitalize on a joint venture in events and gift baskets.

"Wow, that will be amazing! Oh,"—she ruffles through papers on her desk—"that reminds me. There were two voice-mail messages. One is from Mrs. Durham. She has a hair appointment at nine, but she and her husband will be here with Ty at eleven. Miranda and her mom will be here then, too."

At least they're willing to come see me. The timing isn't ideal, putting me behind on decorating if we're a go, but it frees me up this morning to do some online research about poltergeists and revenants, as well as dig deeper about Sam and Tabby.

I want to see if there's anything else out there that's not contained in Mr. Uphill's history or Tabby's diary. Anything that might give me more perspective.

Over the next hour, I discover there isn't much, except the textbook info that local children learn in school and a short newspaper piece from the *Atlanta Tribune*, written a few years back and spotlighting Thornhollow in a Small Town Charm feature. It quotes from Uphill's history, concerning the original founders, Sam and Tabitha, and mentioning their unorthodox manner of life at that time.

Mama calls while I'm scanning the piece. She sounds chipper and tells me Aunt Willa would be proud of my efforts to save the Durham/Burnett wedding. As we chat, I text Brax and Winter.

Imagining Aunt Willa being proud of me, and everything I've learnt the previous night, weighs heavy on my mind. Not blurting out what I heard through the hedgerow last night, and the entries I read in Tabby's diary, sits on my tongue, wanting to break free. The curse was referred to in one entry but not explained, nor was there information on how to break it outside of performing a weird sacrifice that I'm so not doing.

As I was hanging up with Mama, Rosie leaves to check on the flower arrangements and cake for the wedding. She wants to make sure everyone knows nothing has been cancelled. Persephone is nowhere to be found, and I grab some breakfast, replaying Prissy's words in my mind as I return to Aunt Willa's desk with a bowl of warm blueberry cobbler. Tabby does a languid stretch, jumps out of the front window, and climbs the stairs to the bedrooms.

My temper rises hot again, recalling what Prissy and Mr. Uphill discussed. My stomach turns and I shove the bowl away. How dare she try to ruin my family? And he's apparently aided her. Whatever the two of them have done, if it leads me to discovering either was involved with Aunt Willa's death...

The front door opens.

I look up to find Logan peeking his head in and smiling when he sees me at the desk. "Is it safe to come in?"

I sit back and raise my cup. "I've had plenty of caffeine, but not enough sugar. You've been warned."

He wipes his boots on the rug, a few damp leaves sticking to the wool runner, and holds up the town history book. "You left this in my car."

"Thanks for returning it. There's a fresh pot of coffee if you want some."

"Actually, I'm heading to the winery to clean up the speakeasy. That is, if we're still on."

I tap a stack of colored folders on the edge of the desk. "The proposal is ready. I meet with both families at eleven, and I'll call you as soon as I have the official word."

He eyes the stack. "Did you get any sleep last night?"

"A little." No point mentioning my failure at meditating or the sleepwalking. "Mostly running on liquid fuel today."

His grin widens. He deposits the book on the desk and a kiss on my forehead. "See you later."

Once he leaves, I review the outline I've drawn up for the Durhams and Burnetts. Now, more than ever, I'm determined to keep them away from Priscilla.

Still stewing, I hop up and grab a paring knife from the drawer. I head upstairs to the trunk and what waits inside.

Tabby sleeps on top of it. I close the door and she slits her eyes open.

"I appreciate you letting me read your diary," I tell her, "but we're not leaving this room until I have answers."

She yawns, stretches, and eyes me with a half-lidded gaze. I sit on the edge of the bed across from her and give her my stony face.

If cats can roll their eyes, I'm pretty sure that's what she does. Leisurely, she jumps off the chest, goes to the window seat, and begins to clean her whiskers.

My stomach tight with frustration, I wonder if throwing her in a tub of cold water might make her talk. Maybe I can withhold food. Find catnip and drug her with it. There has to be a way to make her talk.

For long minutes, we sit there eyeing each other, neither ready to give in.

"Fine, I may not be the torturing sort, but I *will* figure out a way to make you help me."

She pauses in her cleaning to twitch her ears.

"I guess I'll leave you locked in here until you get hungry enough to talk."

Her eyes narrow but she stays stubbornly silent. She lifts a paw and begins to clean her face.

Maybe reverse psychology? I dig out the locked book from inside the trunk. "I don't want to ruin this, but if you plan to die here without talking to me, I have no choice. I'll have to force the lock open. I'll even remove the bed so you don't have a comfortable space to lie down while you waste away in here."

Her tongue halts in midair. She glares at me as if suggesting I'm an ungracious brat.

I'm pretty sure I know what she's thinking. "I do appreciate your distraction with Prissy last night, and I know you're doing what you can, but it's not enough. I'm not kidding when I say I will keep you locked in here until you tell me what's going on verbally with all of this, or you go...*poof.*" I make an exploding motion with my empty hand.

She sets down her dainty paw. I swear, I hear her sigh. "The curse prevents it, lassie."

The lilt in her voice is soft, nasally from her snout, but *hallelujah*, I've finally gotten something out of her.

"The curse that causes men to die if they marry a Holloway woman?"

She starts to nod, and then her head snaps rigid as if frozen. Still, I see confirmation in her eyes. There's also pain. Whatever the curse involves, it must control her somehow and inflict pain when she talks about it.

Another thread of information though. This is good. "Okay, I get it. If you talk about the curse, it freezes you and inflicts torment. That makes sense about why you don't—or can't—answer my questions." I fiddle with the paring knife, "Let's try a game. Yes or no—is my name Avalon? Blink once for yes and two for no."

A gleam chases away the pain in the golden orbs. Slowly, she blinks once with extreme deliberation.

This might work. "Is Prissy a witch?"

Two blinks. That's a no.

"Did she kill Aunt Willa?"

A long pause, hesitation evident, and then...

One blink, followed by a second.

A no, but it seems like it's not actually a no.

"Did Preston Uphill?"

A second pause, less hesitation, before her lids dip twice in quick succession. Definite no.

"Did Calista?"

Anger sparks behind her eyes, turning them a brighter shade of gold. I hold my breath, waiting as she appears to struggle against the curse. Her body trembles, her lids dipping ever so slightly.

Yes.

"Thought so." Grabbing both the book and the knife, I dig

the metal tip into the lock and twist. It doesn't quite fit and I jimmy it around. "Uphill wants this property, Priscilla wants to bankrupt the business because Aunt Willa is so loved in this community. They couldn't figure out how to get rid of her, could they?"

The metal lock fights me. The cat face on it looks like it's glaring at me. I look up and see Tabby's eyes dance. Blink.

Yes.

I remember the section of Uphill's town history about the last of Samuel and Tabitha's descendants—my family. Just as he and Prissy discussed last night, we're nearly gone. There was a footnote in Uphill's history, claiming Samuel's children with his first wife flourished and thrived, spreading to various parts of Virginia, Tennessee, and here in Georgia.

"Did Uphill steal Aunt Willa's key?" I ask Tabby. "Is he the man you were referring to the other day?"

This must have to do with the curse because Tabby's body goes rigid once more.

The tip of the knife snaps off. Releasing a grunt of frustration, I slam my hands on the book cover. "I need to read this, don't I?"

One blink.

"Uphill took the key to keep me from discovering the truth about him?"

Blink.

My phone, resting on the bedside table, buzzes and lights up with Winter's number. As I answer, she launches in before I can even speak. "A revenant needs a master to control it. This is serious magic, Ava. You need to be careful."

I assume from this she got my text and the information I told her Persephone offered me. "I know who the master is," I tell her. "What I need to know is how to stop her."

"The master or the ghost?"

"Both, either. If I break the connection, will Calista's ghost move on and leave the rest of us alone?"

"Most likely, but not necessarily. She could end up in a kind of limbo and continue haunting this ex-boyfriend of hers."

Perfect. "Do you know any spells for opening a lock?"

Winter half hesitates at the abrupt change in subject matter. "'Open sesame' usually works, especially if you have sesame seeds and are a witch."

"Seriously?"

"Seriously."

I laugh, but it's without humor. "Seeds I can get." I eye Tabitha. "The witch part might be tougher."

"No worries. I'm on my way."

She's such a good friend, but this is my mess to figure out. Mine to clean up. It's especially mine to revenge. "Halloween—Samhain—is only a few days away. You can't leave the store and your sisters. They need you."

"I'm getting on the first broomstick out of here with their blessing. I'll see you soon."

A joke about riding her broomstick dies on my lips as the connection is broken.

I toss the phone on the bed and squeeze the book, as if I could somehow make it explode and release its secrets. The blue leather squeaks, quarrelsome at the treatment.

"How does Uphill know about this book?" I'm only musing out loud, but Tabby's tail flicks back and forth as if she wants to answer. Her head and body remain rigid, and I know that although she is fighting the restrictions of the curse, she desperately wants to tell me everything.

I pick up the knife and strike the lock with the butt of it. Nothing happens, and I do it again, anger boiling in me. A ghost that Priscilla somehow raised and now has under her command killed my aunt.

How am I going to prove that? More importantly, how am I

going to find the key Uphill buried in his backyard? If I can't get this book open, I may have to go digging for it.

Bam bam bam. I take my anger out on the lock, swearing at it, and at the same time asking for God or anyone else who might have some power to give me a freakin' break.

The book sails off my lap as if yanked by invisible hands, and smacks into the closet door before flopping to the floor.

Tabby jumps and looks at me. Slowly, I stand from the bed and stare at the book. Did I cause that, or is Calista here?

No cold breeze or laughing—I believe the house is protected from her, somehow, but I'm jumpy enough to be worried anyway.

Tabitha and I exchange another glance, and together we slowly approach the book. "You're a witch, right?" I ask the cat.

One blink.

"Cool. I have an idea." Bending down, I take her paw. Setting it on top of the book, I hold her gaze. "Aunt Willa, if you can hear me, I need your mojo. Persephone? You, too."

Persephone appears, her gaze floating between me, the cat, and the thick book. "What are you up to? Whatever it is, why don't you wait until Winter gets here?"

"There's no waiting. We do this now." Placing my hand on the book, I close my eyes and pretend I'm Winter. I can see ghosts and I understand talking cats—it's really not hard to imagine I'm a witch. Aunt Willa seems to have had a few magical inclinations, and I'm sitting here with my shapeshifting ancestor and a spirit guide. It can't hurt to try, right?

"Open sesame," I murmur under my breath.

Without warning, the book shakes and trembles, the leather groaning under my hand and Tabby's paw.

My eyes fly open and we look at each other, the book.

I demand louder this time, "Open sesame!"

The book tries to jerk away and I press down on it, keeping it under our ministrations. It snarls.

I snarl back.

Persephone floats in closer and I feel the slightest warmth on my shoulder. I glance over to see her touching it, and even though she's a spirit I actually feel the slightest bit of pressure. "Try again," she says.

Once more, I pour everything I have into my words and my touch. Imagining Tabitha, not as a cat but as my ancient grandmother. "Open sesame," I say calmly.

The book howls, gives one final shudder, and the lock clicks open.

Chapter Thirty-Five

T he Durhams and Burnetts arrive on time and I seat
them around Aunt Willa's desk. Rosie gets everyone a
drink as I make small talk.

The book is back in the trunk and I can't keep from thinking
about it, even as I launch into my sales pitch. I skimmed
through pages and pages of spells, charms and hexes. There
were journal entries stating the outcomes of various spells, ways
to communicate with ghosts, and tips and tricks for keeping
those around you blind to your magical gifts.

The grimoire did not belong to my aunt, nor Tabitha. If I
was to believe the hard-to-read flourishes on the inside of the
title page, the book was, in fact, written by the most unexpected
person in this whole scenario. I still haven't wrapped my head
around it and have no time to put the pieces together at the
moment.

Miranda looks three shades too pale, Ty's fingers interlaced
with hers. She won't meet my eyes as I hand out the proposals. I
make my voice as confident and upbeat as I can with all the
chaos in my brain.

Resuming my seat in Aunt Willa's chair, I silently call on her spirit to aid me as I walk the group carefully through the details of moving the wedding and reception to the vineyard. There are numerous questions, mostly by the Durhams, and I answer them succinctly, squashing Myra Durham's numerous concerns and assuring all that I can pull it off. With forced confidence and abundant smiles, I hope to convince them, as well as myself, that I have everything under control.

My proposal to join the Durham candy empire with the Cross Winery is the final icing on the cake. At first, Mrs. Durham, with her silver blond hair and expensive Burberry suit, refuses the deal outright. Her husband, in John Lennon glasses and wool coat with patches on the elbows, pipes up for the first time. "The idea has merit. I'd like our VP of marketing to look it over and propose something more formal."

This earns him a glare from her.

I direct them to the hastily thrown together spreadsheet at the back of the packet. "I'm not a financial wizard, but preliminary numbers for a joint venture of wedding packages combining specific award-winning boutique wines and your high-end chocolates suggest a ten percent profit increase in direct sales for nine out of twelve months next year alone."

"This is all hypothetical," Mrs. Durham challenges.

Mr. Durham uses a chubby finger to adjust his glasses. "I'll have our CFO examine the numbers and confirm."

Another glare that nearly scalds me, and I'm only a bystander.

"Aren't all great business adventures hypothetical in the beginning?" I counter with another smile, thinking of Queenie and my mother. Both of them had a dream and did the work to make it a reality. "These numbers are based on the amount of weddings over the previous years' averages, so they're a decent predictive bottom line as far as the market goes. And honestly, it doesn't take an expert to see the advantages both of your businesses will reap. The fact you're in each other's backyard, with the vineyard and the chocolate manufacturing warehouse within ten miles of each other, keeps overhead and transportation costs low."

Dead silence falls. Mrs. Burnett reaches out to pat Miranda on the arm. "Please, Myra, business aside, can't you work it out with Helen so our kids can get married in a beautiful setting?"

The candy empress presses her ruby red lips together, and her husband nudges her, pointing to my spreadsheet. "We could double this easily."

Another twitch of her lips, then a long-suffering sigh through her nose that reminds me slightly of Tabby.

Ty leans forward to look around his father at her. "For me, Mom?"

He's really asking for Miranda, and her gaze flicks up to mine with hope. I subtly wink at her.

Mrs. Durham's eyes soften and she turns them on him. "Fine, we'll hold the ceremony and reception at the winery,"—now her gaze turns to me and hardens—"but I withhold agreement on the business proposition until I see more in-depth investment proposals."

Relief swims through me. I glance at Miranda. "Are you happy with this change in venue?"

The hope in her eyes has bloomed into full-on joy, a touch of her normal color returning to her cheeks. "Can you really pull this off?"

Ty's gaze asks me the same. He has hope, too, but like his bride he's afraid it won't work because of Calista.

A warmth invades my chest. I love weddings, love the emotion of love. I've missed the event side of wedding planning, and the happiness I feel when I sketch a dress. I vow to do more of both. "Yes, Miranda, we'll pull it off, but the final word is up to you and Ty. Is this what you want?"

She squeezes Ty's hand. He kisses her temple. "More than anything," she says softly.

"Awesome. We'll get to work immediately." A part of me is happy that Logan is already working on the speakeasy. As the parents rise, we exchange handshakes. Mrs. Burnett hugs me and thanks me profusely, asking if there's anything she can do.

"Just take care of our bride for me," I tell her.

"I can do that."

Seeing them to the door, I wish them all a good day and reassure them once more. Then I pull the bride and groom aside. "Would you two stay for a minute to go over a few tiny details?"

Ty and Miranda look surprised but agree. After they say goodbye to their parents, they follow me to Rosie's side of the first floor where a fire crackles in the hearth. Rosie hustles around, grabbing papers from her desk.

Once we're finally alone, she positions Ty and Miranda in front of the fireplace and gives them each a detailed list, as if this is actually what we are going to do—review everything. "We want to, um...practice the vows and make sure we have everything covered," she tells them.

"Isn't that what the rehearsal is for?" Ty asks.

On cue, Reverend Stout arrives.

"Yes." I search for the right words to alleviate their confusion as Rosie shows the pastor into the room. "But since I won't be there, and I haven't been in on all the planning, I'd appreciate it if you'd run through the vows here for me, right now."

I'm not taking chances. If this house is protected from Calista, and I believe it is, I'm taking matters into my own hands. "Trust me," I tell him with a big smile. "Practice makes perfect."

Protected in Aunt Willa's house, I watch Ty and Miranda smile happily into each other's eyes, as Reverend Stout walks them through their wedding vows.

Chapter Thirty-Six

When I arrive at the speakeasy an hour later, I'm amazed at the transformation Logan has already pulled off. Things are clean, organized, and I jump in to help him finish wiping down tables and chairs.

We unload Aunt Willa's van, where I've stowed the decorations. Rosie pulls up shortly after me, bringing a bunch of the fall flower arrangements and endless strings of lights.

Being the helpful assistant she is, she's created a map for where everything should go based on the description I gave her of the place. She gives Logan and I each a copy, and with just a few tweaks we go to work.

Mrs. Cross shows up around three, bringing her sommelier and some of the other staff. I can see she's impressed, even though she tries to keep it off her face. Several employees of the Durhams deliver chocolates and I put all of them to work lining up various bottles of wine to go with the candies.

The tables take on a life of their own, decorated with fall leaves, tiny pumpkins dipped in white sparkles, and an assortment of fine china and crystal glasses.

Logan repairs a weak spot in the dance floor, while Rosie

and I set up a table and a few minor decorations to the DJ area so it flows easily with the rest. The DJ himself will set up later that evening.

Logan and one of the winery employees erect tents outside the back doors of the speakeasy, and more tables and chairs are set up under them. Rosie takes over those decorations.

Mrs. Cross and her sommelier stock the bar, and Brax and Queenie check in with an update on the food preparation for the reception. The country club chef has offered to help Queenie create much of the original menu.

At three-thirty, Mrs. Cross lets us know she has no intention of attending the parade and tells us she'll continue working on a few of the last-minute items while we go. She and I discuss her concerns about the tour on Sunday, and then Logan and I leave her and Rosie and head back to town.

On the way, Logan teases me. "I know you have a lot on your plate, but that's the least amount I've heard you talk since you got here."

I admit to being very distracted, and he has no idea of everything I've discovered in the past day. "I could use a clone," I tell him, wishing my latent magical abilities could conjure one, but as soon as I think that, I remember Calista and decide it's probably not a good idea to venture into that territory. With my luck, instead of cloning myself, I'd raise a ghost. Or a dozen.

He continues to make easy conversation, letting me know he's impressed with what I've pulled off in the last couple of days. Normally, I would appreciate it, but today all I want to do is get through this parade and back to figuring out how to prove my theory about Aunt Willa's death.

Everyone is already in the church parking lot when we arrive, and we're directed to the front of the parade line-up. Mama flies by, leaning down into the convertible to give me a quick kiss before she flutters away, her speech notes clutched in her hand.

Logan pulls out a couple of magnetic signs from the trunk and puts them on each side of the doors. He motions me to get in the backseat and sit up on the convertible top area. Then teases me about practicing my parade wave.

I consider giving him a finger wave instead, but the enthusiasm of everyone around me buoys my spirits. I laugh, giving in, and pretend for a moment that I'm an elegant princess waving to the common folk. This draws laughter from Logan, and I smile secretly to myself.

At the direction of Reverend Stout, we begin the trek to the start line downtown. As we pass Mr. Uphill, waving his arm in a "let's go" gesture at the lineup, I send him a glare, but he's too busy to notice. Prissy's nowhere in sight, and it's a good thing. Thankfully, the poltergeist/revenant seems to be absent as well.

As we reach the start of the parade, I see hundreds of people lining Main Street. "This event has grown since the last time I was home during Fall Fest," I tell Logan.

"Another reason to come home more often," he counters.

There's a podium stationed to the side of the start line, and the sound system emits various squeaks and squawks as someone adjusts it while Mama stands waiting to announce the kickoff of the fall festival.

She's smiling and happy, and that makes me happy as well. I'm not sure whether to tell her my theory tonight or wait until after the festivities are done.

Eventually, the sound system is working properly, and Mama raises a hand in the air. The crowd begins to fall silent, stretching out block after block down the road. She clears her throat and begins to speak, the last of the conversations falling quiet.

"Welcome," she says, looking out over the crowd.

Many folks respond in kind, raising their hands to wave. There are many smiling faces, and the general air is one of anticipation and joy.

"What beautiful weather we have today," Mama says, and another response from the crowd echoes off the Main Street buildings, affirming it. "This whole weekend is going to be an amazing time, and we welcome our out-of-town visitors as well as those who live and work here in Thornhollow."

She knows just how to pause and let the crowd do their thing before she resumes her speech. "Today is the parade, and tonight I hope to see all of you at the hotly contested homecoming football game."

A huge roar goes up from different areas on both sides of the street. There's cat-calling, whistling, and clapping. Mama smiles and eventually gets the crowd to settle once more. "Tomorrow will be a beautiful day for shopping and sightseeing. Remember all of the fall festivities going on in the various locations. Be sure to pick up your map"—she points to a stack of brightly colored fliers on a folding table near the podium—"and if you don't get one here today, you can find them at any of our downtown shops."

She glances at her notes, but I don't think she needs them. She's memorized all of this, and some of it has come through years of kicking off this weekend. Seeing her in the limelight and how much she enjoys it makes me smile.

"On Sunday, we have the much-anticipated Peaches and Pumpkins Wine Tour that passes through our very own award-winning Cross Winery. Bring the kids and take home all your wine needs for the coming holidays."

A small cheer goes up, and a few people near the start of the parade wave at Logan. He waves back.

Mama grows serious. "If you'll all humor me for a moment, I want to thank my daughter, Ava." She does a Vanna White impression with her arm, sweeping it over to me.

I feel a hot flush hit my cheeks as everyone turns their attention to me. Her voice continues to echo out of the speakers and down the line. People stand on tiptoes and try to get a better look at me. "It's been a rough week for our family, and Ava has stepped up beautifully to help out with the fall festival after the death of her aunt. She's running The Wedding Chapel and handling a very special wedding tomorrow in the midst of all of this. The wine tour on Sunday at the Cross vineyard is going to be even better than Willa planned, all thanks to Ava. Please visit the winery to show your support, and say hi to my daughter if you have a chance. Thank her for her help in keeping the fall festival alive this year."

The cheer that goes up is louder than any of the previous ones. I feel like sliding down into the back seat, especially when Logan turns to look at me with admiration. He motions me to stand up and acknowledge the cheering crowd. I wave him off, a rush of modesty making my cheeks hot.

But then I look at Mama and see her motioning for me to do the same, and I hesitantly get to my feet, standing on the nice leather of the seat and doing a rather weak parade wave to thank the crowd for their generosity.

I wish Aunt Willa was here more than anything, and her absence makes tears come to my eyes. This would be her night if she were alive, and I would still be back in Atlanta, eating cold pizza and getting ready for another dull weekend in my apartment.

I stop with the princess wave and give a genuine one instead, like she would do, and people return it. As my gaze scans the crowd, I see one person who's not waving.

Priscilla Barnes. My attention stops on her and she turns, melting into the crowd.

As the applause and cheering die down, I resume my seat and smile at Mama. She smiles back and nods. Once again she commands the crowd and they fall silent. "And now...what you've all been waiting for! The kick-off to this year's Thornhollow Fall Festival! Let the parade begin!"

Logan shifts the car into gear, and we are just about to pull forward when a police siren cuts through the air. People in the crowd turn to one of the side streets where a cruiser rolls up, lights flashing.

Logan hesitates, and Mama shoots me a confused look. Two police officers exit the car and race toward the raised podium. They both look slightly abashed, but one of them—the one who arrived the first day I was here when I fell off the porch—comes forward and says something under his breath to Mama.

Her hand flies to her chest and she takes a step backward. She shoots a fearful glance at me.

Instinctively, I jump out of the car and hustle to the podium. The police officer steps toward her and the mic picks up his voice now. "I'm really sorry about this, mayor," he says, "but I'm afraid I have to take you in."

I hop onto the edge of the podium, nearly falling, but managing to scramble up. "What are you talking about? Take her in for what?"

I realize too late that my voice is clearly coming through the speaker system, the agitation echoing back to my ears.

He pinches his nose and then gently holds out his hand toward Mama. "The autopsy is done on Willa, and I have to bring you in for questioning."

There's murmuring in the crowd, and my stomach falls. "What in the world for?"

He sighs dramatically, and stares Mama straight in the eye. "You are a suspect for the murder of Wilhelmina Duchamp."

Chapter Thirty-Seven

At the station, I pace back and forth near the front desk. Reporters crowd around the station entrance, but the woman in charge, Sandy, according to her name tag, is keeping them out.

Thank goodness for small mercies.

Thornhollow's police station is relatively small and run down. It stinks of old coffee and body odor, and Sandy fields calls and directs people to various forms to fill out or to the chairs in the waiting area, all the while eyeing me behind her bright purple reading glasses.

I don't know what happened with the parade, but Logan is here with me, ready to defend Mama. While he's behind a closed door with Detective Jones, Doc arrives with the results of the autopsy. He greets me and plops into a chair, asking me what happened downtown.

I recite a brief summary, trying to keep my shaking fingers under control. "I hear you had a thing for my aunt." I want to sound accusatory, as if I might get him to confess to her murder, but mostly I sound hoarse. Tired. Scared.

"I lov…" He clears his throat. "Your aunt was a light in my life."

"Did you see her the day she died?"

His face contorts. "We were supposed to have a nice supper, then your mama asked her to eat with her instead. I never got to tell her…"

His voice hitches and I see him blink back tears.

Crude. I feel terrible guilt at suspecting he might have killed Aunt Willa. "I'm sorry. This must be as hard on you as it is me. She never mentioned you were a thing, so I was surprised about your relationship."

He withdraws a white hanky and dabs at his eyes. "I thought we were going to have many more years together. Should have known something was up…she kept acting strange that week."

"Strange how?"

"She seemed distracted, worried. Kept talking about her assets and making sure her business affairs were in order. I thought she was just having a bad week. We all go through that at times. Friends and family get ill, pass on. Makes us face our mortality, you know?"

"Do you know who might have done this to her?"

His mouth hardens and he shakes his head. He motions for me to sit next to him and then he shows me a copy of the autopsy.

The crux of it makes me shake as he explains. "Looks like Willa was not dead when she fell in the water of the creek," he says. "It appears she may have had a heart episode, but it doesn't fit the normal parameters of a heart attack."

I give him a blank look, my mind a mess.

"Something happened with her heart," he continues in the simplest terms possible, "but the coroner isn't sure what."

"Great," I say, exasperated. "Then why have they arrested Mama?"

He glances at the paper, even though I sense he doesn't need to. "There was a bruise on the back of her head. It wasn't visible underneath her hair initially, but from the size, location, and angle, it suggests someone wacked her at the base of her skull, causing her to fall in the water." He clears his throat. "Ava, the coroner believes the person held her face in the stream and drowned her."

"Oh my heavens." I clutch at my heart and reel back. He grabs on to me to keep me from falling out of the chair. "That's horrible!"

I let myself cry and Doc gives me time to recover, offering his handkerchief. Sandy hands me a paper cup of water, but my hands shake so violently I can't hold onto it.

While I've seen the amount of power Calista has, and I was nearly convinced the ghost had done the killing, now I'm not sure. Calista can knock heavy vases off a table, fiddle with the electricity, cause the plumbing to flood, but could she pick up a rock and hit a woman in the back of the head? Could she physically hold someone's face underwater and drown them?

I find it doubtful, but I know someone who could…someone who wants to destroy us and get rid of Aunt Willa's business.

And she's no ghost.

Mama was the last to see Aunt Willa alive so she's the prime suspect. Since it's Friday night, no one can get her out on bail until Monday. I can't exactly point the finger at Prissy unless I have solid evidence. Overhearing her and Mr. Uphill in the yard last night is not enough. I've watched crime shows and know hearsay isn't proof. Also, I have to go about this very carefully, or my mother could be going to prison for a long, long time.

Doc tries to talk to me, comfort me, and insists that we'll find a way to clear Mama's name.

"I want to see her," I tell him.

Logan and Detective Jones emerge from the back of the station.

"I'm sorry, Miss Fantome," Jones says. "You can't until her bail hearing on Monday. It'd be best for you to go home."

I wonder if she's scared. I know she's horrified at this as much as I am.

Jones leaves.

"Logan?" I'm hoping for some kind of reassurance.

He opens his arms without a word. A sense of foreboding swamps me and I fall into his arms. His hug is solid and warm, reassuring me. Tears come again, fear and anger spilling over. I'm beyond embarrassed to cry into his shoulder, but it seems everything is out of my control.

He pats my back and assures me everything is going to be okay. I melt into his broad chest, and I hear him and Doc exchange several comments about what's going on, but it's background noise. I tune into Logan's heartbeat, feel it bolstering me.

Eventually, he guides me out the door, Doc on our heels, and the two men exchange a couple of words about what they'll both do to help Mama. All I can think about is trying to get a confession out of Prissy, how to stop this runaway train before it goes any farther.

Logan doesn't let go of my hand as he drives me back to the house. Two of the reporters from the station follow and he puts the top of the convertible up to shield me. Doc also follows and arrives shortly after we do.

Inside, Rosie rushes to me, having heard about what happened, but it's Logan who explains everything to her.

In the middle of this, Winter arrives. We hug it out but I don't cry, even though a flood of tears threaten again. I introduce her to the others and bring her up to speed.

Logan, Doc, and Rosie give us privacy, heading into the other room to discuss the autopsy. Winter sits at the table in Aunt Willa's chair, two cups of steaming tea appearing with a wave of her hand, and the two of us put our heads together.

"Who's the revenant's master?" she asks.

Everything in me has gone very still. Tunnel vision, maybe. I sip the tea and feel whatever magic she's infused it with working to unknot the tension in my muscles. "Her name's Prissy Barnes. She's probably having a good time right now. I doubt she was trying to set up Mama, but somehow she managed it."

Winter places her hand over mine. "Is there a way we can lure her here to the house?"

Winter is a powerful witch and knows what she's doing. Whatever she's planning? I'm in. "I'll drag her here kicking and screaming if I have to."

Logan's voice comes from the doorway, and I jump, realizing he was eavesdropping.

"Ty Durham's going to be honored at the football game tonight. I'm guessing she's there."

Winter glances from him to me, as if asking if he can be trusted. I give a nod. "Do what you can to get her here, and I'll take care of the rest. Where is this armoire with herbs in it?"

I take her upstairs and show her the hidden cabinet. She begins pulling out various dried flowers and sniffing at bags.

"What are you going to do with that stuff?" I ask.

She hands me a bag of what looks like cloves. "Truth serum. Got any good brandy?"

Alcohol, the best truth serum known to man—or witch—in this case.

In the kitchen, she shows me how to make the serum, insisting I do the work myself to make it more potent. "You're the one who needs answers," she tells me. "You have to create the potion for her to give them to you."

The mixture bubbles and turns an interesting shade of lime green. "Is that it or do we need something more?" I ask.

"All we need is the person with the truth locked inside her."

I nod, knowing exactly how to get Prissy to The Wedding Chapel.

"Come on," I say and motion to Logan as I hustle through the front area.

Chapter Thirty-Eight

He drives us to the game, and I ignore the looks that people give me, the way they speak behind their hands and point. A few are bold enough to actually ask me if Mama really killed my aunt, and it's all I can do not to punch them in the face.

Instead, I call on the good old Holloway backbone, straighten myself up, and paste on a smile. "My mother wouldn't hurt anyone, and y'all know that. Enjoy the game."

It doesn't take long to find Prissy holding court with some of her friends behind the bleachers. She's smug as she sees me approach.

Logan, a few steps behind me knows the plan. He brushes my lower back in support. I stop several feet from her cluster of friends. "Could I speak to you for a moment in private?"

She exchanges looks and a snicker with the two women from the country club. "Whatever for?"

"I'm sure you know what happened earlier."

"Your family is a disaster," she says. "Get to the point, Ava. What do you want?"

I move away from the group, into the shadows of the bleachers. After an annoyed pause, she follows.

I glance at the ground and act embarrassed. "Aunt Willa's business is done, finished. I can't handle the wedding tomorrow and I want to get out of this town. I hate it here. I thought maybe you could..."

"Could what?"

"Are you interested in buying out the business?"

A sudden silence falls, even the crowd in the stands seeming a million miles away. In the weak light, I see her scan my features.

"I know you don't need the business name," I rush on, "but Aunt Willa has a ton of supplies, and all the weddings that are coming up at the end of this year and into next. I'd like to turn all of those brides over to you so I don't leave them hanging."

I have her complete, undivided attention now, and the way the corners of her mouth turn up tell me my bait is working. "I'll consider it."

"I don't have time, Prissy. I want to get out of town tonight. If you want it, we need to make a deal now."

"Pushy," she snarls. She starts to walk away. "I said I'll think about it."

"I can have Logan draw up the agreement tonight."

That stops her. She turns back, one of her eyebrows lifts.

I motion at him. "I'm selling the house, too. Aunt Willa left all of it, including the house, to me, so I can do whatever I want with it. If you don't want The Wedding Chapel's business, I'll have to turn it over to Rosie."

"Rosie?" Another snort. "You can't be serious."

"What choice do I have? It's you or her."

She's playing hard to get, but I know I've got her. Acting as if this is an inconvenience, she shrugs, her focus landing on Logan. She licks her lips. "I suppose I can take a few minutes to go over the paperwork with you. I need to be back for the varsity game, though, y'hear?"

I return to Logan's side and soon we're in his car, Prissy following.

Inside the house once more, not only is Winter waiting to help me but so is Persephone. Tabitha circles Winter's ankles, her golden eyes sparkling and gleaming. She's ready to break more than one curse tonight. But the only one I care about at the moment is this connection between Prissy and her ghost.

I drop a light kiss on Logan's cheek and tell him to go home.

He insists on staying. "I can help," he says under his breath in my ear.

Goose bumps race over my skin at the warmth of his breath. "I'm going to need your help over the next couple of days, but right now the best thing you can do for me is go home, or go back to the game. Act normal, and if anyone asks you what's going on with me, pretend you have nothing to do with me now. Distance yourself from us."

His face goes hard, a muscle in his jaw jumping. "Get real, Fantome. That's the last thing I intend to do."

I squeeze his arm. "Trust me. This is all part of my plan. I promise I'm going to fix everything."

He shakes his head and argues with me for another minute, until Prissy comes through the front door. She's gliding on air.

She eyes the front windows and I see the wheels in her head turning as she inventories what she wants from my aunt's displays.

"Please, Logan. I have this under control and I'm not alone." I point to Winter. I'm not sure if she's sent Rosie home or on some errand, but I'm sure the two of us, along with Persephone, can handle what's about to happen. "I'll talk to you as soon as I'm done here."

Prissy strolls over to us, and his jaw works overtime a little more before he nods and stalks out.

"What's with him?" she asks offhandedly. "Isn't he staying to draw up the contract?"

I motion her toward Aunt Willa's desk. "He'll be back in a jiffy with it."

Winter enters the room and the two exchange a look.

"Let's get started," I tell Prissy, getting her to focus again on me. "So we can get you back to the football game."

Chapter Thirty-Nine

✿❋✿

P rissy takes a seat across from me. She continues eyeing
things, as if she owns them already.

"Do you know anything about your family history?"
I ask. From the kitchen, I hear the whistle of the tea kettle.
Winter and Tabitha wait in there.

Prissy looks at me as if I'm wasting her time. "What
about it?"

Answering a question with a question. Hmm. "You may not
have realized it, but you're a descendant from Samuel Thornton
and his first wife Redemption."

She stares at me half a second too long before she shrugs.
"So what? I thought we were going to talk about the business."

I take a seat in Aunt Willa's office chair, leaning back and
steepling my fingers in front of my chest. Winter warned me
earlier to be careful with her. If Prissy's capable of raising a
revenant ghost and bend it to her will, we don't know how
strong of a witch she is. "Redemption was a member of a Salem
family of witches. Did you know that?"

I see the fact register and she starts to reply. Then she steels
herself and makes a scoffing noise in the back of her throat

before she looks away. "Ava, you've lost your marbles. How many weddings are on the books for the last of the year?"

She wants to pretend innocence, but I'm sure she's heard this version of history before even though it's been all but erased from the town's archives.

"Redemption's family left Salem during the trials, even though they'd blended in so well with the Puritans no one realized they were the ones performing magick. Redemption's family members were masters at the Craft, and were able to conceal their real nature and turn all eyes on innocent people."

Winter comes in with two cups of steaming tea, saying nothing as she sets them on the desk for me and Prissy. There's a third cup as well, but it's empty. "Thank you," I say to her.

Priscilla eyes her cup with disgust. Maybe she's a coffee person. "I'm not here for tea and a history lesson. I couldn't care less who my ancestors are. I live in the present, and I want to hear your proposal about selling The Wedding Chapel."

I blow on the hot liquid, mostly out of spite to force her to cool her heels. "I'm gonna get to that in a second. Hear me out okay?"

The tea is just right and I sip leisurely. Her eyes have gone hard, and she's glaring at me.

"Redemption even fooled Samuel for a long time after they met and married. Eventually, he found out and left her." I tap the book of spells, now unlocked, that sits on the edge of the desk. "From this account, it appears he tried his best to get the kids away from her as well, but she turned the town against him."

Prissy looks up at the ceiling as if asking a higher power to help her with her patience. "Get on with it, already."

"It was my great-great-grandmother, Tabitha, a good witch by the way, who helped Sam escape before the town could hang him. Your grandmother, his first wife, cursed him and his future offspring, while putting protective charms on their children so he and Tabby could never get them away from her."

As I drum my fingers with one hand and sip my tea with the other, Priscilla dons a face that tells me I'm crazy. "You're all about witches, aren't you? You and your crazy aunt."

I bristle, but refuse to rise to the bait. I pull Tabitha's diary out of a drawer and set it on top of the spell book. "Tabitha Holloway's diary"—I tap the worn leather—"states they never stopped trying to get Samuel's kids away from Redemption, but her magic and influence were too strong. So, he and Tabby made a home here, naming the town Thornhollow and creating their own family and a supportive environment free to everyone, no matter their religious beliefs or their walk of life."

She huffs, coming to her feet. "Are you selling me the business or not?"

"Relax." I wave her back into her seat. "I just found it interesting that we're very, very distantly related, and the history in my grandmother's diary differs so much from the one we've grown up with, don't you? The other fact never mentioned is that Preston Uphill is also a descendent of Redemption and Samuel."

Her avarice rises to the surface and she sits down on the edge of the chair. "What kind of profit margin am I looking at for the next six months?"

At least she's sitting. Behind her in the shadows, Winter motions at me to get her to drink the tea. Tabby slinks into the room and hides under the desk. "You're looking at ten thousand dollars or more, based on the current number of brides." I've made this up off the top of my head, but it makes her eyes glow. "Knowing your aggressive promotion strategies and networking abilities, Prissy, you can probably make more than that."

The corners of her mouth curl. I raise my cup as if in salute.

"Seems like this calls for congratulations. You're getting what you always wanted."

Reluctantly, she raises her cup and gingerly taps it against mine. She barely takes a sip, but then seems to find it appealing and drinks more. "This is good stuff. What's in it?"

"Honey, brandy, some vanilla."

"Brandy, huh? That must be the interesting aftertaste I'm getting."

I see the potion going to work, her muscles relaxing. The tightness around her eyes dissipates and she sighs.

"I can't wait to get out of this town," I lie. "But it makes me happy that Aunt Willa's business will continue."

She nods, and then the truth serum kicks in. "I have no intention of keeping this business up and running."

Her eyes widen in alarm. She clamps her jaws together, shocked at her confession.

I press back in the chair and rock. "I'm not surprised. You've made it clear you have a different way of doing things. I'm just relieved that our brides won't be left out in the cold."

"I'm gonna suck them for every penny I can get."

Again, shock registers on her face and she covers her mouth with a hand.

Now that the potion is full strength, it's time to get to the truth. "So you've been dabbling in magic?"

She starts to shake her head to deny it, but then says, "I couldn't resist. I tried a silly beauty spell I found on Pinterest one day and it worked. I had to try more."

"Latent magickal power runs in your blood, thanks to Redemption. I have the same, apparently, with Tabitha's blood. Unfortunately, playing with the spirit world is dangerous business, and you're no Redemption I'm afraid. Was it your intention to force Calista's ghost to kill my aunt?"

Now she does shake her head. Her cup slams into the saucer hard, spilling what's left onto the desk. "I had nothing to do with her death. I mean, I messed with Calista, but her spirit wouldn't willingly respond to my requests."

My eyes go to Winter. She scowls. This must be bad news. "But the ghost killed Aunt Willa?" I confirm.

She tries again to silence herself, but the truth tumbles from behind the hand over her mouth. "I think she did."

I wonder how in the world I can prove my mother's innocence if a ghost murdered my aunt. I already had my suspicions, but now it's confirmed and I'm more worried than ever. "You *think?* Don't you know?"

She gives a half-hearted shrug, and I understand this is the truth—she's not sure.

And that means...

She's not the one controlling Calista.

I mentally curse. Who then?

Must be Prissy's partner in crime. Now I'll have to deal with him.

At least there's one thing I can do right now—break the family curse. "In this spell book that belonged to Redemption,"—I slide the diary away and tap the leather-bound tome again—"I found a way to lift the curse on Samuel and Tabitha's progeny, but it requires the blood from the last descendants of both Samuel and Redemption."

Her eyes go wide. "What are you talking about? You're not suggesting..."

She knows exactly what I'm suggesting, and fear ripples across her face. I pull out Aunt Willa's letter opener, the tip sharpened and gleaming under the overhead light. "It's just a little prick, Prissy. You'll hardly feel it."

"No, no... I...I don't do blood magick." She jumps up, but before she can run out of the room Winter flicks her fingers and Prissy falls back into the chair, unable to move.

I lift a brow at my friend.

She shrugs. "Binding spell. I'll teach you how."

Prissy fights as, against her will, we draw blood from one of her fingers and let it drip into the empty cup. Winter adds the assortment of herbs we gathered and the powder we ground up. "Now yours," Winter says to me.

Tabby circles my feet and I have an idea. I jab one of my fingers with the letter opener. "I think we should throw some of Tabitha's blood in, too, just to be safe."

The cat meows loudly, and I assume she doesn't want to have her blood drawn either—or maybe she thinks it's good idea. Hard to tell.

Two drops fall into the cup and I straighten, licking my finger. "Is that enough?" I ask Winter.

The air around us seems to shiver. She looks toward the shadows, and I see her frown again.

"What is it?" I ask.

"The wards..."

A man's voice from behind us interrupts her and sends shivers down my spine. "I wouldn't do that if I were you."

I jerk around and see an ugly black gun pointed at me.

Chapter Forty

❦

Preston Uphill moves faster than I expect of a man his age.

Winter, still holding the cup and Prissy's arm, isn't quick enough to defend herself as he attacks.

I scream as he hits her in the head with the gun and she crumples to the floor. The cup crashes near my feet, the handle breaking and the contents spilling.

I take a swipe at Uphill but he dodges, kicking the chair Prissy is in and sending her tumbling into me. We topple backward, and in the frenzy I hear Persephone yell at me to get up.

With Winter out cold, the binding spell breaks. Prissy rolls, pressing the arm of the chair into my rib cage and making me gasp. She comes up on hands and knees, and I fight with the chair to get it off of me.

Preston points the gun at both of us. "We're not breaking any curses tonight," he snarls.

As Prissy gains her feet, she acts relieved to see him. "Thank goodness you're here. They took my blood!"

She lifts a fingertip to show him her injury, like a child wanting their mother to kiss a booboo. The barrel of the gun follows her as she steps closer to him. "Stay over there," he demands.

Prissy's confusion is evident as she looks back at me. I'm torn between helping Winter and stopping Preston.

"What's with the gun?" she stage-whispers. "That's a little much, isn't it?"

"Shut up." He waves the weapon, motioning her to return to me.

Rib screaming in pain, I gain my feet. Winter is breathing, and I pray she'll be all right. I grab Prissy's wrist, hauling her behind me. "Put the gun down, Mr. Uphill. Everything's fine. There's no need for any violence."

He checks out the books on top of the desk. I notice Tabby's hiding under it again. A disgusted sigh escapes him as he fingers Redemption's grimoire. "You broke the lock. Figures. I knew Willa had this, but it belongs to *me*." He taps the gun against his chest.

"It should be burned," I murmur. "The magick in there is bad stuff."

He acts like he didn't hear me. "All of this,"—he motions with his free hand, encompassing the house—"belongs to me. I'm the *true* descendant of Samuel and Redemption. I'm the only one who's carried through on the revenge Redemption deserved to mete out on your family. You and your meddling aunt should have never been born."

"And yet, here I am."

His smile is wicked. "It ends here."

"But Preston…" Prissy is still in disbelief, disengaging my hand from her wrist so she can step forward. "I thought we were in this together. What's wrong with you? Why are you acting like this?"

His thin face draws into a haughty expression. "You are so easy to manipulate. All I needed was to appeal to your worth-lessness, make you feel like the only way to prove yourself in this town was through your business. Setting you up for killing Willa, and now Ava, was entertaining, but not exactly challenging."

Her mouth falls open. "What are you talking about?"

With the gun, he motions at Winter. "Who's that?"

Prissy, somehow believing they're still partners, tells him. "She's a witch, like Ava. The tea she made me... I spilled my guts about things. And then she did some kind of spell that kept me from leaving."

"Friend of yours?" he asks me.

Probably not after I've nearly gotten her killed. Unfortunately, impending death is not off the table yet.

Prissy steps toward him again and uses a cajoling voice. "There's no reason this has to go bad between us. I can help you take care of her and Ava, too."

He shakes his head as though exasperated. "I don't need your help, you stupid girl. I have everything under control. The scene is already set—there was a fight between the three of you, I heard shots and ran over to see what was going on. After I kill you in self-defense,"—he points the gun at Prissy—"I'll blame the other two deaths on you as well."

The gun turns toward Winter. I scream and jump between her and the gun, and just as I do Aunt Willa appears next to Uphill.

"Preston! You scoundrel. Don't you dare! You can't do this in my house against my niece."

Uphill startles—can he hear her?—and flinches. Seeing my opportunity, I jump, reaching for the gun.

Just as I do, a cold gust of air blows past my face, pushing hair across my eyes. Calista's laughter rings out, sending chills down my spine.

I see a ghostly swish of energy as she attacks Aunt Willa, and when I grab the gun it fires.

Chapter Forty-One

❧❀❧

White hot pain rips through my shoulder. At the same time, Tabby launches herself onto Uphill, digging her claws into his thigh.

He screams; the gun points up to the ceiling, and Aunt Willa and Calista wrestle in the air as I stumble back, tripping on the chair leg.

Falling, I try to avoid Winter's body and shout for Persephone.

What did Uphill do to the house to reverse Aunt Willa's protection charm? I land hard, my injured arm unable to support me, and I tumble over the broken cup near Winter's body. Blood drips, there's a sizzle, and a fireball explodes around us.

The bright light floods the room, partially blinding me as I roll away. As if everyone else is suddenly frozen, time seems to stand still.

Through the icy whiteness around me, I can actually see Calista's full form, fingers reaching like claws toward Aunt Willa's face.

Prissy, who took cover behind the other office chair, is

huddled into a ball. Uphill and Tabby are frozen in their *pas de deux*.

A dark, wiggling thread of energy floats out of Calista's chest. It's barely visible, but I can trace it through the air between us.

It doesn't lead to Prissy, but to Preston Uphill.

He's the revenant master.

Knew it.

The light is sucked out of the room as quickly as it came, and time restarts. Uphill finishes his scream, Tabby's claws tearing through his pants into his skin. Prissy mews like a kitten in fear.

Instinctively, I push myself toward the desk. My shirt's sticky from the blood. My right arm tries to reach for the letter opener but doesn't succeed, the searing pain turning to numbness.

I swing my left hand around, thanking Tabby for keeping Uphill distracted. I grab the letter opener.

The gun comes down, Uphill grabbing Tabby and wrenching her from his leg. Instantly, I'm as angry as I've ever been. Tabby may be in cat form right now, but she's my grandmother, and I'm not about to let anyone hurt her.

The gaping distance between us is too much for me to gain my feet and make it to that thread between master and ghost. I'm a poor thrower even with my right hand, but I have no other option.

With Uphill's gun swinging around to point at me and him ready to pull the trigger, all I can do is rear back and throw the letter opener as hard as I can.

It flips end over end through the air in slow motion. At the same time the gun goes off once more.

Aunt Willa throws a ghostly hand out toward the bullet that exits the gun, my undivided attention locked on it.

The knife cuts through the connection between Uphill and

Calista. Calista stops in mid-strike, ready to hit my aunt in the face with her clawed hands, and all the rage drains from her.

A ripple of energy rockets through the space. I drop to the floor, dodging the bullet but feeling the breeze as it spins past my temple.

The front door crashes open.

As Uphill yells in frustration at missing me, and Calista waivers in and out of a ghostly form, Logan sprints into the room. He takes everything in in a quick second and jumps on Uphill, knocking him to the floor.

Persephone appears behind Logan, and I dive for the gun as it spins away.

Calista turns and looks at me, her face drawn in sadness and horror. "I'm sorry," she says in a shaking voice. "I never meant to..."

Logan has Uphill's hands pinned behind his back, one of his knees digging into the man's side. He glances my way, and I see his face morph as he registers the gunshot and my bleeding shoulder.

"I know," I say to Calista. To Logan, I try to reassure, "I'm okay. We just need to..."

The room spins and I pitch forward, catching myself on the edge of the fallen chair back. Black dots dance in the corners of my eyes, and Persephone says, "Looking a little peaked there."

My stomach heaves, eyes attempting to roll up inside my head. I fall sideways to the floor once more, the world tilting on its axis.

Before the world goes dark, I see Calista attack Uphill.

Chapter Forty-Two

I wake up at the clinic sometime later. Doc has bandaged my arm and the police are there to take my statement. The bullet went through, Doc tells me, and I guess I'll live.

The police arrested Prissy Barnes and Preston Uphill, and Detective Jones instructs one of the cops on duty to dig up Preston's yard where I direct them to.

Uphill is in the county lock-up, and Prissy has pinned everything on him, Jones tells me. Apparently, neither mentioned the ghost, but I don't care—Mama is free. She stops at the clinic to check on me, and after a bit I send her home to get some rest.

They find Willa's key, and, bonus, the rock used to hit her on the back of the head.

Winter shows up a bit later. My friend came out of last night's fiasco okay and refuses to be examined. She got Calista to cross over permanently, and we both hope to never see her again. Knowing I'm in good hands between Logan, Mama, and Rosie, she kisses my forehead and leaves to return to her home in Raven Falls.

Doc keeps me at the clinic the rest of the night and I'm anxious to go home, but Mama is busy getting the delayed parade back up and running. As I walk out of the clinic, feeling a touch of deja vu, I find a red convertible waiting for me in the parking lot.

Logan piles out, smiling. He opens the passenger door, and although I'd like to come up with a snarky comment I simply smile back and get in. He hands me coffee and a bag from Queenie's. Suddenly, I'm ravenous. He updates me on a few details about the day's events while I stuff my face.

He drops me at Aunt Willa's so I can freshen up and change clothes while he checks on a few things at his office. Not easy to do with my arm still somewhat out of commission, but I manage. Doc loaded me up with painkillers and sleep aids, which I don't think I'll need. I'm planning a full-on crash later.

I send Winter a quick text once I find my phone and tell her thanks for all her help. She replies immediately to ask how I'm doing. I tell her that I haven't been this good in a long time, and that's the truth, plain and simple.

After I finish with her, I call my dad. "Just checking on you," I tell him.

"My baby." His voice is a deep baritone and I can sense his smile in it. "How are you?"

"I have a lot to tell you. Do you think you can visit me one of these days?"

"Say the word and I'm there."

"I'm moving to Thornhollow," I blurt.

There's a weighted silence. "Your mama finally blackmail you into moving home?"

"There's a lot more to it, I'm afraid."

"I'm real sorry about Willa Rae. I always liked her."

The front door opens and Logan peaks in. "You coming?"

"I've got to run, Dad. I love you."

"I'll see you in a few days."

After I hang up, I go to Logan. "Do you think after everything that's happened, that someone else could take my place?"

He shakes his head and holds his hand out. "Are you kidding? You're the star of the show."

News travels fast in our little town, and I have no doubt everyone has heard the story about what happened last night. Reluctantly, I walk toward him, take his hand, and let him lead me back out to the convertible.

The sun is warm on my face as we resume our place at the front of the line, even more people gathered along the sides of Main Street, talking, laughing. It takes more work today, but Mama finally silences the majority of them and launches into a new speech.

I'm only half listening, my shoulder beginning to throb as the morning's pain meds wear off, but I feel clear-headed. I'm relieved to have uncovered the truth about Aunt Willa's death, as well as some truths about other things. There are plenty of people in the crowd beaming at me, and I sense a collective relief from them as well. So many people were touched by Aunt Willa's life, and knowing she's received justice in death seems to make them happy.

"I want to take one moment to recognize my daughter," Mama says.

There's some clapping and a few cheers and people wave to me up and down the blocks.

"If it weren't for her, I might not be standing here talking to you today. If it weren't for her and her…"—she clears her throat —"gifts, my sister's murder might have gone unsolved. I can't think of anyone Willa Ray would want more than Ava to continue her tradition and to lead this parade."

Cheers ring out, and without any prompting, I stand. Heat rises up my neck into my cheeks, but I accept the praise graciously. Logan places a finger and thumb between his lips and gives a sharp whistle. I can't help but laugh.

"I want to request a favor of all of you," Mama continues. "If you have a chance to speak to Ava at any point this weekend, or support her efforts with the wedding this afternoon or the wine tour tomorrow, please do so! Tell her we need her, make her feel welcome, and maybe, just maybe, she'll move back home."

Laughter and a smattering of clapping echoes through the crowd. Someone yells, "We need you, Ava!"

Someone else joins in. "It's time to come home!"

I recognize those voices, one being Braxton and the other his mother. I roll my eyes and sit, and with a few final words from Mama the parade gets under way.

Once the parade is over, Logan and I head to the speakeasy to put the finishing touches on things before the wedding. His mother gives me a nod of approval over the chocolate and wine baskets, and soon, the florist, Queenie, and Reverend Stout arrive. Even Mama stops by to see if I need helped with anything.

At 4 p.m. on the dot, Miranda walks down the aisle we've created between rows and rows of chairs filled with people. Ty and his groomsmen look stunning against the backdrop of the valley, the rich red satin of the bridesmaids' dresses popping against the natural fall colors surrounding us.

The vows are said without any drama other than a few tears from various folks in the crowd. It truly is a stunning wedding, and throughout the reception I receive numerous compliments. I make sure that everyone knows it was a joint venture and I couldn't have pulled it off without the Cross family, Rosie, Queenie, and all the others, including my mother.

I keep it to myself that Ty and Miranda are technically already married, thanks to Reverend Stout and my sneakiness the day before. I needed to be sure they had at least that in case Calista was able to ruin today.

Throughout the wedding and reception, I spot a few extra ghostly guests and toward the end of the night, I pull Miranda to a quiet spot outside and give her a message from her father who is on the other side. "He's so proud," I tell her, and her eyes go wide as saucers.

"You see him?" she asks in a whisper.

I nod. "He loves that you pinned one of his army medals on your crinoline."

No one but me, and probably her mother, know it's there. Her eyes swim with happy tears. "Thank you," she says, placing her hand on my arm and squeezing. "Just...thank you."

After the bride and groom head off on their honeymoon, the guests begin to file out. Mrs. Cross receives plenty of inquiries into buying the chocolate and wine baskets and mentions to me in passing that we better have more for the tour tomorrow.

Ty's mother seems pleased as well, and at one point lets me know she'll be looking into my proposal in more detail in the coming weeks now that the wedding is done.

I'm dead on my feet, and looking forward to a long night in bed, when Logan saunters over and asks me to dance. "You deserve at least one trip around the floor," he says. "And I'd be honored to be your partner."

Across the way, I see Braxton smile at us. Rhys is with him, and they both wink at me.

Logan is dressed in a nice suit and fits right in with the wedding guests. His hand is warm as I take it. "You never told me how you knew I was in trouble last night."

He gently leads me to the dance floor, taking me in his arms and swaying to the slow tune the DJ is playing in order to wind up the reception. "I had a visit from a ghost."

I lean back slightly, my brows jumping up in surprise. "You saw a ghost?"

He chuckles so softly I barely hear it above the music, but I feel it in his body, a warm sensation spreading throughout mine in response. "She was kind of odd, and I thought maybe I was losing my sanity, but she said you needed help."

"What did she look like?" I'm pretty sure I know the answer.

He glances away, his brows knitting in a frown. "She had weird orange hair, and bright green and blue clothes on, tons of makeup, and, honestly, she had a really snotty attitude. She looked like that one actress who used to be on and old sitcom series my grandma watched back in the day."

I sigh, leaning into him a little more and enjoying how safe he feels. "She's not really a ghost, per say. More of a spirit guide."

"Oh, you mean like your guardian angel or something?"

"Or something." Instinctually, I lean my head on his chest and close my eyes.

"I was on my way when I heard the gunshot." He strokes my hair. "Thought I was going to lose you again."

My knight in shining armor. Or more like a three-piece suit.

It's a beautiful night. The Snow White wedding is a blessed success with plenty of pumpkins, love, and joy.

And no poltergeists.

Chapter Forty-Three

A fter a full eight hours of uninterrupted sleep, I wake to find Mama downstairs brewing coffee. I must look a sight because she gives me a double take when I wander into the kitchen.

The cats greet me, and I feed them as she pours me coffee. My arm aches and I massage the area around the wound gently.

"Logan was over a little bit ago and asked if we want to go over the will today," she says as I plunk down at the table and sip the delicious brew.

I was hoping I might see Aunt Willa yesterday or last night, but I was too tired by the time I got home at 1 a.m., after cleaning up the speakeasy, to really tune into the spirit world. "It's Sunday, why aren't you at church?"

She shrugs. "Today, I want to spend time with my daughter. I think the Lord will understand after what we've both been through in the past few days."

She joins me at the table and we sit and discuss normal things, like the weather, the homecoming game—we won—and my plans for staying on.

I don't feel the usual abrasiveness at discussing this with her today. I feel a real sense of belonging, a new sense of purpose. I share this with her and see her beam with happiness. "But," I amend, "if I move back, you have to promise not to drive me nuts about my life and what I'm doing with it."

She makes a motion of zipping her lips shut, locking them, and throwing away the key. Which reminds me, "Did the police give you Aunt Willa's key back?"

She shakes her head. "For now it's evidence, so until Uphill has his day in court, we probably won't see it."

I don't really need it now, but for sentimental purposes I'd still like to have it. "What's going to happen to his bed and breakfast? Has anyone been over there to help his guests?"

"Actually, yes. Queenie was over this morning bright and early to make sure they all had breakfast, and most will be leaving today after the wine tour. She said that Braxton and Rhys have their eye on the place." She scoffs without any energy behind it. "Like they need another business!"

True, but... "I think that'd be awesome." It would be so fun to have my bestie next door. "They could live there, and I'm sure they could hire more help for the other businesses."

"Well, Preston Uphill doesn't have any relations that I know of," she says. "So his property might be up for grabs at some point, if he's convicted."

"*When* he's convicted," I correct.

Taking my coffee, I go upstairs, enjoy a shower—tricky with my bandaged arm—and spend a little extra time on my hair and makeup.

Not that I'm anticipating seeing Logan or anything. Actually, I dread going through Willa's estate documents, but doing it with Logan will ease the pain for me.

The temperature is in the low seventies as Mama and I make our way across the street to his office. A few leaves blow across our path. He and Moxley greet us at the door and Logan ushers us inside.

The office is like him, beautiful in a down-to-earth way. Warm browns and rich oranges, a few splashes of ocean blue. He leads us into a room with a large wooden desk and comfortable chairs. Moxley climbs into a dog bed in one corner.

As Logan reads through my aunt's last will and testament, I feel slightly stunned. It's not a complete surprise that I inherit the land and the business, but apparently there are more secrets to be revealed.

Logan reaches in a drawer and hands me a safe deposit box key. "This might explain what she was doing with her money. She gave it to me the day she died, said to keep it for you as part of the will."

Mama and I exchange a look. Twenty minutes later she's convinced Mr. Randall, the bank manager, to open up and let us in. Being mayor does have perks, I guess.

The safe deposit box contains a number of important documents, including the missing bank statements that I never got back to looking for. There's also a fancy business card with a woman's name and phone number. None of us know Gloria Stone, so I dial the number and hold my breath.

She doesn't seem surprised when I tell her who I am, and I love her French accent as she responds. "Willa told me you'd be coming soon to see your creations."

"My what?"

"How soon can you get here, *cherie*?" She reels off directions to a place several miles outside of town. "It would be best if I show you what we've accomplished so far."

Logan joins Mama and me as we head out of town. Mama is as confused as I am about where this trip is leading.

Inside a rambling two-story farmhouse, Gloria offers us tea and cookies in her fashionable sitting room. She's a slight woman with fine features and is dressed in a wool skirt and silk blouse.

Sunlight pours through a set of double doors on the far end

of the room, overlooking a sweeping view of a tree orchard. "It's nice to finally meet you," she says to me. "Your aunt thought you had what it takes to be a fashion designer with a line of unique wedding dresses, and I have to agree."

I grip my tea cup. "Sorry. I don't think I follow."

She rises from her lushly upholstered chair and goes to an antique French-style desk. The metal handle on one of the drawers clanks as she opens it and withdraws a slim stack of papers. "Even as a young girl, you had an eye for design."

Returning, she hands the stack to me. I set down the cup, realizing these are copies of the dresses I sketched as a teenager.

Mama and Logan lean in to see as I flip through the dozen or so sketches. "She gave you these?" I ask.

"Those and her life savings."

Mama gasps, a hand going to her lips. "Oh my."

I still don't connect the dots. "Why?"

Gloria smiles and motions for us to follow. Mama, Logan, and I all exchange a look and then do so.

The house looks like it's straight out of a Home and Garden spread. Everything is high-end and immaculate, but I hardly notice as we walk through the first floor toward the back door. Anticipation of what's waiting for us makes my pulse skip.

"My partner Joseph and I believe in the value of handmade items," Gloria says, "and we only work with a select few Georgia designers whom we feel have a nostalgic Southern bent and, most importantly, understand this momentous day in a bride's life."

We exit the house and walk along a meandering collection of stones covered in moss. Arriving at a large metal building, the entrance is a beautiful sliding barn door with a painted illustration in apothecary script, announcing *Miss Jasmine's Boutique Bridal Designs*.

"Wait." I stare at the sign. "I know who you are. Southern Bridal carries your Josephina vintage line."

A gleam lights her eyes. "One of my favorites, the first I ever designed."

Inside, there are numerous wedding dresses on display in various stages of completion. A man with a bushy mustache and headband looks up from a sewing table and waves.

We wave back, assuming that's Joseph. Gloria leads us to a display area on the left and I can hardly believe my eyes. "Willa had us construct several prototypes from your drawings."

Hesitantly, I walk forward to the beautiful dress closest to me. With tears in my eyes, I gently brush my fingers over the luxurious silk material, noting the incredible hand-sewn beading along the neckline.

Gloria turns the dress form to show me one side. She draws back a lace panel to reveal a set of tiered layers of white satin underneath.

"The hidden staircase," I murmur.

"What?" Mama asks.

I can't believe it—my vision has come to life. "I designed this one after reading *The Hidden Staircase*." At Mama and Logan's blank looks, I explain. "The Nancy Drew story?"

"The lace is detachable." Gloria demonstrates. "And the top 'stair' contains a pocket for the bride, just like Ava's model."

Logan smiles. "Practical."

"Isn't it? I hate clothes that don't have pockets." I fiddle with the satin to peek inside. The lining is perfect and elegantly trimmed with more tiny beads. "Every bride needs a discreet one in her dress."

As though my aunt is there with us, I feel her arms go around me. I sigh. "Thank you, Aunt Willa."

In my ear she whispers, "I love you, Ava. I'll always be with you."

Chapter 44

⁂

That afternoon the wine tour goes off without a hitch, except that I keep catching sight of odd energies hanging around. None of them fully form or engage me, and I'm so busy I leave them alone. They return the favor and do the same for me.

My arm feels better. I mixed up some of the herbs from Aunt Willa's cache according to a recipe Winter sent me, and it's allowed me enough pain relief that I don't need the strong meds that Doc prescribed. He and I have a lunch date to get together and talk about my aunt next week, and I'm looking forward to it. Tomorrow, Mama and I plan to finish off the funeral arrangements, and I'm sure Aunt Willa will make an appearance again.

By noon, the Cross family estimates the tour guests have already doubled this year, and I have to admit part of the reason is me. Not because I've done a better job than Aunt Willa did in previous years, but because I've become somewhat of a celebrity after taking on Preston Uphill.

Many folks stop to ask about my injury and if I'm hanging around to take over the business. It feels good to say yes, and think about the wedding dresses that are all mine and may sell next year to help bring in money to buy back the mansion.

Some of the people who approach inquire about hosting events for them around the holidays. There's no shortage of parties around here during this time of year, and Rosie delights in setting up appointments and penciling things into our calendar all afternoon.

That evening, as the tour winds down, Logan brings me a glass of peach wine and a few stolen chocolates. Moxley, his constant companion, moseys over to sit at our feet. We toast and Logan congratulates me on all of my hard work, including solving Aunt Willa's murder, pulling off the wedding, and having a successful tour. "I hear you're sticking around for a while."

I bite into a chocolate cordial and smile. "Seems I have a few good reasons to."

He winks at me. "Better than the ones in Atlanta?"

Gloria Stone gave me the names of buyers interested in my line of dresses, one of them in Atlanta. I have the feeling I'm going to be busy between keeping The Wedding Chapel going and this offshoot of my childhood dream. "I'll probably have quite a few trips in and out of the city," I tell him, "but home base for Avalon Wedding Designs is going to be here."

"I like it," he tells me, clinking his glass against mine. "You know, the Winter Ball is only six weeks away. The chamber will need someone to take care of the details."

"Rosie can do it."

He frowns, chewing a bite of candy slowly. "It's a big deal, think she can handle it?"

"I hope so since I plan to go as a guest, not the event coordinator."

He grins slyly. "Did someone already ask you to the dance?"

"I'm keeping my dance card open."

He sips his wine and eyes me over the rim. "I happen to be

looking for a date, myself, and was hoping you might do me the honor."

I finish the chocolate and sigh with delight. Suddenly, I remember Aunt Willa's entry in her ledger—Candy Lane—and understanding hits me like a lightning bolt. "You're Candy Lane."

"What?"

"CL. The letters...she reversed them. Cross, Logan. I thought she was referring to Ty Durham, but it was you, wasn't it? You're a candy nut. What did you hire Aunt Willa to do for you?"

His eyes go wide at my announcement, and then he looks away. "It's nothing."

"You weren't surprised at all that I have her gift, were you?"

A heavy sigh. "Nope."

I can't remember what service was listed next to his moniker and start to ask again when he waves a hand. "Look, it was no big deal. I was trying to decide whether to stay here or leave town, maybe head to Atlanta like you did. She pulled a few cards, looked into her magic ball, and told me if I left I'd have financial success, but if I stayed I'd find my soul mate." His gaze comes back to mine. "Corny, right?"

Corny, but the fact he chose love over money makes me want to kiss him.

I catch his mother eyeing us from several feet away, where she's chatting up several country club board members. She doesn't look exactly happy about our relationship, but she's not staring a hole through me either, so I smile at her and turn back to her son. "Is that true? Did she really tell you that?"

"She did. I think she knew a lot more than she ever let on."

Boy, did she. I have the feeling I've only uncovered the tip of the iceberg. I bend over and scratch behind Moxley's ear. "I want to design a new dress to wear for it. The ball."

"I can't wait to see it."

I step closer to him and touch his cheek. "Maybe I'll make a matching tie for you."

Grinning, he kisses me. I kiss him back.

Later, after Logan drops me at home, I go to the trunk and pull out a few of the items under the watchful eyes of Tabitha. She should be able to talk now about the curse, or anything else, but she stays silent. I don't pressure her, but I do promise to restore her original home one of these days, as soon as I've paid off the house loan.

Aunt Willa's spirit doesn't make an appearance, but I do feel her presence. Tabby paws at a scarf in the trunk, so I take it out and wrap it around my neck. The faint scent of my aunt's perfume engulfs me and I hug the material to my nose, breathing it in. I move Teddy and the crystal ball downstairs and place both on her desk. I swear I see a vision inside ball. Possibly a trick of the light, but it looks like Logan holding me in his arms.

Braxton shows up, tells me I look fabulous, and together we head to the Thorny Toad.

That evening is filled with odd encounters and interesting discussions, and I even get my cards read by a gal who specializes in tarot. There are a few cards that look like bad news, but overall the reading sounds positive.

Several people ask me about seeing ghosts—Miranda spilled the beans on me about her dad showing up at the wedding, and the word is out. Here, no one seems all that surprised, and I wave it off, telling them that was Mina the Medium's area of expertise.

I have so much on my plate to think about, I'm not sure I want to establish being a medium right now, regardless of the fact I see plenty of spirits hanging around the place. There's so much to learn, and I don't know what I'm doing yet, so it's best to stick with what I do know.

I'm sitting with Brax and twin sisters who are private investigators. They have some pretty strong psychic abilities, and I enjoy hearing about a few of their cases but pray they're not picking up stuff about me. Although, at this point, what do I have to hide?

The four of us are deep in conversation when someone stops at our table, dressed all in black with a hat and sunglasses. The woman shifts the glasses and stares down at me. "May I speak to you in private, Miss Fantome?"

It's Logan's mother. I'm gobsmacked; she's the last person I expect to see here.

Excusing myself from the table, we meander to a booth in the far back corner.

Although it's shadowed here, she still seems nervous and doesn't take off the hat and sunglasses. They're so dark I can't believe she can see much. "I don't want anyone to know I believe in this stuff." She glances around, ducking her head slightly even though no one's paying any attention to us. "But I need your help."

Oh boy, this should be good. "Of course. I'll do what I can. What is it?"

From her bag, she removes a necklace and lays it on the table between us. "This was my mother's."

I glance at the embossed gold locket, feeling a repressed, heavy energy encircling it. I wait for her to explain more, but she simply looks at me as if that explains everything.

"What about it?"

"It's cursed."

I sit back, as if getting too close might allow it to rub off on me. I'm done messing with that stuff. "Cursed how?"

"It's not the necklace itself that I need help with."

I'm confused. "Then what is it?"

She shifts uncomfortably, wringing her fingers and shooting another anxious glance at the bar. She lowers her voice. "The ghost inside."

I pause. "There's a ghost *in* the necklace?"

She nods and stiffens her back slightly as if in defiance. "Yes, an evil spirit put there to stop it from harming me."

I feel like I've entered the Twilight Zone again and shake my head. "And what exactly do you want me to do about it?"

She leans forward and lowers the glasses so her eyes make contact with mine. "I want you to get rid of it, and it has to be done before the Winter Ball."

I'm pretty sure I don't want to know, but I ask anyway. "And why is that?"

"Because if you don't, the two-hundred-year-old curse that's contained him this long will expire, and the ghost is going to be free." She grabs my hand with a claw-like grip. "It's going after Logan, Ava. You have to save my son."

Magic & Mistletoe, Confessions of a Closet Medium, Book 2

Coming September 2020!

About the Author

Nyx Halliwell is a writer from the South who grew up on TV shows like Buffy the Vampire Slayer and Charmed. She loves writing magical stories as much as she loves baking and crafting. She believes cats really can talk, but don't tell her three rescue puppies that.

She enjoys binge-watching mystery shows with her hubby and reading all types of stories involving magic and animals.

Connect with Nyx today and see pictures of her pets, be the first to know about new books and sales, and find out when Godfrey, the talking cat, has a new blog post! Receive a FREE copy of the Whitethorne Book of Spells and Recipes by signing up for her newsletter http://eepurl.com/gwKHB9

Books by Nyx Halliwell

Sister Witches Of Raven Falls Mystery Series

Of Potions and Portents
Of Curses and Charms
Of Stars and Spells
Of Spirits and Superstition

Confessions of a Closet Medium Cozy Mystery Series
Pumpkins & Poltergeists
Magic & Mistletoe (Fall 2020)
Haunts & Hearts (Spring 2021)

Once Upon a Witch Cozy Mystery Series
If the Cursed Shoe Fits (Cinder) May 2020
Beastly Book of Spells (Belle) August 2020
Poisoned Apple Potion (Snow) October 2020
Red Hot Wolfie (Ruby) January 2021
Hexed Hair Day (Rapunzel) April 2021

Connect with Nyx today!

Website: nyxhalliwell.com

Instagram: https://www.instagram.com/nyxhalliwellauthor/
Email: nyxhalliwellauthor@gmail.com
Bookbub https://www.bookbub.com/profile/nyx-halliwell
Amazon amazon.com/author/nyxhalliwell
Facebook: https://www.facebook.com/NyxHalliwellAuthor/
Twitter: @HalliwellNyx

Sign up for Nyx's Cozy Clues Mystery Newsletter and be the
FIRST to learn about new releases, sales, behind-the-scenes
trivia about the book characters, pictures of Nyx's pets, and
links to insightful and often hilarious *From the Cauldron With
Godfrey blog*!

Dear Reader

I hope you enjoyed this story! If you did, and would be so kind, would you leave a review on Goodreads and your favorite book retailer? I would REALLY appreciate it!

A review lets hundreds, if not thousands, of potential readers know what you enjoyed about the book, and helps them make wise buying choices. It's the best word-of-mouth around.

The review doesn't have to be anything long! Pretend you're telling a friend about the story. Pick out one or more characters, scenes, or dialogue that made you smile, laugh, or warmed your heart, and tell them about it. Just a few sentences is perfect!

And if you're interested in crystals, psychic readings, energy healing, astrology, or past lives, please visit https://crystalswithmisty.com/ to find out more about how these all-natural, fun services can help you live a calmer, healthier life!

Blessed be,

Nyx 🩶

PNR & UF by Misty/Nyx

Paranormal Romance

Witches Anonymous Step 1

Jingle Hells, Witches Anonymous Step 2

Wicked Souls, Witches Anonymous Step 3

Dark Moon Lilith, Witches Anonymous Step 4

Dancing With the Devil, Witches Anonymous Step 5

Devil's Due, Witches Anonymous Step 6

Dirty Deeds, Witches Anonymous Step 7

Wicked Wedding, Witches Anonymous Step 8

Urban Fantasy

Revenge Is Sweet, Kali Sweet Urban Fantasy Series, Book 1

Sweet Chaos, Kali Sweet Urban Fantasy Series, Book 2

Sweet Soldier, Kali Sweet Urban Fantasy Series, Book 3

Sweet Curse, Kali Sweet Urban Fantasy Series, Book 4

Paranormal Romantic Suspense

Soul Survivor, Moon Water Series, Book 1

Soul Protector, Moon Water Series, Book 2

Cozy Mysteries (writing as Nyx Halliwell)

Sister Witches Of Raven Falls Mystery Series

Of Potions and Portents

Of Curses and Charms

Of Stars and Spells

Of Spirits and Superstition

Confessions of a Closet Medium Cozy Mystery Series

Pumpkins & Poltergeists

Magic & Mistletoe (Fall 2020)

Haunts & Hearts (Spring 2021)

Once Upon a Witch Cozy Mystery Series

If the Cursed Shoe Fits (Cinder) May 2020

Beastly Book of Spells (Belle) August 2020

Poisoned Apple Potion (Snow) October 2020

Red Hot Wolfie (Ruby) January 2021

Hexed Hair Day (Rapunzel) April 2021

CPSIA information can be obtained
at www.ICGtesting.com
Printed in the USA
LVHW080812030622
720418LV00008B/266